From Wags to RICHES

by
Cate Miller

ILLUSTRATED BY AMY KLEINHANS

www.orangehatpublishing.com - Waukesha, WI

From Wags to Riches
Copyright © 2022 Cate Miller
ISBN 9781645383185
First Edition

From Wags to Riches
by Cate Miller

For information, please contact:

www.orangehatpublishing.com
Waukesha, WI

Cover art and illustrations by Amy Kleinhans
Cover design by Kaeley Dunteman

From Wags to Riches is a work of fiction. Names, characters, places, and incidents are either the product of the author's imagination or coincidence. Any resemblance to actual persons, living or dead, businesses, businesses, events, or locales is entirely coincidental. The character of Kind Kirby is the one exception to the above disclaimer. The actual Kind Kirby spent his first four years in a cage in a puppy mill before the author adopted him through the National Brussels Griffon Rescue. The author is eternally grateful to the NBGR for making his adoption possible.

It takes a village to publish a children's book. From Wags to Riches is for all the members of my beautiful village.

Preface

From Wags to Riches is a celebration of my love of dogs. That said, I don't recommend pet ownership for all. The decision to have a pet must consider the wants and needs of humans and animals alike. When adopting any kind of creature, a human is making a commitment to care for her/him for the rest of her/his life. This involves providing appropriate food and shelter; walking, training, and poop patrol for a dog; maintaining litter boxes, crates, tanks, etc. for other types of animals; care when the animal is sick and as the pet ages, or if it has special needs. This can be expensive, so financial ability must be considered as a factor in an adoption. All pets must be provided for in the event of life-changing circumstances such as marriage, a move, a lease that doesn't allow pets, an illness, or a job change. Advance planning is the best policy.

I begged my parents for a dog for much of my youth, but they felt it wouldn't be fair to a dog to be home alone so much with them both working and me at school. We finally adopted our first dog when I was ten, and I've rarely been without a dog in my life ever since then. I've loved them all, some of whom were rescues, some who were abused, and some who came from legitimate breeders.

Pet ownership, although it can be immensely rewarding, is not the only path to pet companionship. If you want a dog, but for whatever reason cannot have one, there are still many avenues to having animals in your life. Consider adopting a pet you can have like a bird or a hamster. Befriend someone with a pet and contribute to caring for their animal(s). Give food or treats only as allowed by the owner. Take a neighbor's dog on walks. Clean a litter box for a cat owner friend. Volunteer at the Humane Society or another animal sanctuary. Visit animal sanc-

2

tuaries. Animals are to be treasured whether we have them in our homes or not. Open all your senses to the glorious joy of nature that surrounds you every day!

Table of Contents

ILLUSTRATIONS

WAGS'S MENTAL AGILITY ACTIVITIES

Cast of Characters

Wags

A cute and sassy Yorkie, Dog #63 at The Dogg House

Nomad

A stray dog, Wags's friend and confidant

Kind Kirby

Senior resident of The Dogg House

THE TIGGYWIGGLES

Hortense Tiggywiggle

*Chief Financial Officer (CFO) of Frenchy's Dog Food,
wife of Billy, mother of Beatrix and Augustus*

Maxibillion X. Tiggywiggle, aka Billy

*Chief Executive Officer (CEO) of Frenchy's Dog Food,
husband of Hortense, father of Beatrix and Augustus*

Beatrix, aka Bea, aka honey bunches of groats
Daughter of Hortense and Billy

Augustus, aka Auggie
Son of Hortense and Billy

THE WYSYWYGS

Brambles Wysywyg
Hortense Tiggywiggle's uncle and Walter's brother

Big Mama Wysywyg
Hortense's mother and Walter's wife, a great singer

Toothless Walter Wysywyg
Hortense's father and Big Mama's husband, lead guitarist for his band, Extortionist Love Puppy

Felonius Hunk
The Wysywygs' white bulldog, piano player for Extortionist Love Puppy

THE CRUIKSHANKS

Cookie Fagin Cruikshank

TV spokesperson, co-owner of Fagin's Cars for the Stars, wife of Francis, daughter of Fast Eddie Fagin

Francis, AKA Cranky Franky

Co-owner of Fagin's Cars for the Stars, owner of The Dogg House puppy mill, husband of Cookie

Craig Cruikshank

Francis Cruikshank's nephew

ENDWELL COMMUNITY

Sheriff Dimonte Deck and his drug-sniffing chihuahua, Sarge

Norbert Dingle

Sheriff Deck's husband

Finessa Bopp

Chef/Owner of The Dandy Diner

Faith Carmichael

Owner of Au Naturel Pet Store

Lydia Déjeuner

Dog breeder for the stars, owner of Champion Sir Lancelot Lickalot of Lake Lucy

Chapter 1

The Dogg House

It was a morning born for poets.

Dew bubbled on newly sprouted leaves, releasing a deep, fresh earthly fragrance into the air. Sunlight fluttered through a thin veil of morning fog. All the melodies of nature harmonized at the beginning of a luscious summer morning in Endwell, Wisconsin.

Despite nature's bounty on this glorious day, a six-pound Yorkie named Wags (aka Dog #63) was aggravated and aggrieved. Wags had no family to claim her, no hearth nor home. She was imprisoned at The Dogg House, a puppy mill owned by a disreputable car dealer, Francis Cruikshank, aka Cranky Franky.

The Dogg House was a warren of rusty cages stacked in a weathered, ramshackle barn on the Cruikshank's estate, Fagin's Resort. Located on a golf course just west of Endwell, the house was a gloomy heap of thick, heavy stone intended to look like a castle. It had towers with turrets on each of its four corners and a walled inner courtyard with a gatehouse. Visitors had to use a squawk box to gain entry. Few residents of the town, other than those who worked for the Cruikshanks, had ever seen the inside of it. There were rumors of a dungeon in the basement that were never proven or disproven.

Wags was miffed because three of the dogs had been sold, and therefore freed from the squalor of their environment. She was a handsome dog: perky, with pointy ears, a pert, ink-black nose, and a long, silky coat of steel-blue and golden-tan hair. (According to Yorkie fans, it was hair, not fur.) Cruikshank was a fan of money, not dogs. Wags was a perfect example of her breed, and Cruikshank planned to mate her. Each of her puppies could bring in thousands of dollars. She would be bred for the first time with the revered stud dog, Champion Sir Lancelot Lickalot of Lake Lucy. A criminally cute Yorkie sire, he was in such demand that the tightwad Cruikshank agreed to pay Sir Lancelot's owner $1,000 cash for the opportunity to have Wags mate with him, with no guarantee of success. Cranky Franky thought that this was a sure thing and would get him a faster and bigger return on his investment than most of the businesses on the stock exchange. His snake-like eyes glittered at the thought of the money he'd be making.

Though her situation looked bleak, Wags was a true *magnum in parvo*: a great, big spirit in a small body. She had majestic dreams of breaking out of the dreary puppy mill and going from "Wags to riches." In the meantime, she was just one of dozens of puppy mill residents in a place where there were no amenities, not even for a would-be champion breeder. There was no temperature control in the drafty barn full of cages, so it was

Wisconsin-cold in the winter and practically tropical come summertime.

The rusting, dilapidated wire cages were arranged in stacked columns and rows, a couple dozen in total. The inhabitants were so sweet and pitiful, they could've melted the iciest of hearts. Water and food bowls, which were too often empty, sat haphazardly on newspaper-covered floors in the small spaces teeming with canines. The atmosphere reeked of misery.

There was little peace at The Dogg House. The constant barking, whining, and howling would have woken the dead and buried if not for its remote location. To the east, on the far side of a prairie called Brambles' Sward, was the Tiggywiggles' property, The Wishing Well. The two families who owned the properties were close geographically, but not in any other way.

That morning, the constant barking throughout The Dogg House was a result of food(!), glorious food(!), and the fact that there was never enough of it. This was a recurrent theme at The Dogg House.

Wags was alone in a cage in the bottom row of the tenement kennels, separated from the rest of the dogs, to ready her for her big day coming up. She leaned against the wire mesh of her enclosure while conversing with Nomad, a neighborhood stray who had stopped by to chat while he was out on the prowl for his next meal. He was a white-and-brown, spotted, medium-sized dog with floppy ears, an unruly mop of fur sprouting from his head, and a long tail that quavered tentatively as if he was worried that the sky would fall momentarily. Other caged dogs joined in their conversation.

"I don't see why old Cranky Franky doesn't sell me. Aren't I good enough to get out of this place?" Wags said indignantly.

"That's just the problem," said Kind Kirby, a Brussels Griffon who had been in residence at The Dogg House since his birth four years before. "You're too good."

"So, it's bad to be good?"

"If you want to get out of this joint, yes," Kirby responded. Kirby himself was so irresistible, Cruikshank would not let him out of The Dogg House except for breeding. Kirby's liquid brown eyes, dark-brown smushy-face muzzle, and sweet look of puzzlement would've sold him to the most adamant dog hater. Over the years, breeding Kirby had been a very lucrative business for the miser. Dozens of pups, born with Kirby's princely face on them, had been sold into loving homes for thousands of dollars, but Kirby never knew the love of a human being.

"Cranky Franky has kept Kirby because of his looks," said Nomad. "There must be hundreds of dogs with his face on them."

"Not hundreds," said Kind Kirby modestly.

"Plenty," Nomad responded.

"You *are* a handsome devil," said Wags to Kind Kirby.

"Correction: he's a handsome *angel*," Nomad interjected. "He couldn't be kinder."

"Thanks, Nomad," said Kirby, then he mused, "Oh, if only I were a Tiggywiggle."

"What's a Tiggywiggle?" Wags inquired.

"A wriggling twig?" one doggo wondered.

"A dancing dynamo?" offered a large beagle.

"Nay, it is a fortunate family that made a fortune in the dog food business," said Nomad.

"You don't mean Frenchy's Dog Food?" gasped another dog in reverence.

"Yes, indeed," said Kind Kirby, the elder statesman of the puppy mill. "Once, when Cranky Franky was trying to get me interested in a rather dull old girl, he gave me a bowl of their fine food for encouragement."

"What's it like?"

"It's like nothing you've ever tasted before," said Kind Kirby. "Certainly nothing you've had here. It was so rich and meaty that it restored my faith in humanity that a human could make such phenomenal food for us dogs."

"So, how can we get some?" Wags wanted to know.

"You could pray you get adopted by the Tiggywiggles," Kirby said wistfully. "The Wishing Well, their estate, is just beyond Brambles' Sward in Endwell."

"It must be a far cry from here at Fagin's Resort," Wags said with some resentment in her voice.

"Not so far in miles," said Kirby, "but worlds away from The Dogg House, I've heard."

"If I were a Tiggywiggle, would I get Frenchy's Dog Food?" Wags inquired.

"Oh, yes," Kind Kirby assured her.

"Then I am going to become a Tiggywiggle!" said Wags, resolved in her pronouncement.

"Dream on, my fur friend," said Nomad. "I hear Billy Tiggywiggle, the father, hates dogs."

"But he hasn't met *me* yet," Wags responded. "I'll do more than dream. I'll make it happen!"

Chapter 2

Where There's a Wags, There's a Way

Days went by without a change in circumstance for Wags. Now and then, Nomad wandered by.

"Nomad, have *you* ever had Frenchy's Dog Food?" Wags inquired one afternoon.

"Frenchy's?" he sighed in worshipful awe.

"Yeah, right, so have you?"

"Yes, I have. The Tiggywiggles gave out samples last year at Frenchy's Woofstock. Just between you and me, Wags, it was so marvelous, I snarfed up extra samples from some of those society dogs when they weren't looking. They didn't care; they get it every day. You and your fellow doggos at The Dogg House may wonder where your next meal is coming from, but the Cruikshanks' two fancy Russian Borzois, Anastasia and Vladi, live large."

"It sounds like the Tiggywiggles are generous, for humans. What else do you know about them?"

"I've heard that Mrs. Fedelia Tiggywiggle, who married into the family, grew the business into the conglomerate it is today."

The Tiggywiggle empire began humbly with Whiskers Tiggywiggle, the local butcher known for his impressive red walrus mustachio and for giving tasty scraps of meat to neighborhood dogs. The entrance to his shop became overrun with dogs, so his savvy wife, Frenchy, a native of Paris, began cooking up the scraps, canning them, and selling the food to neighborhood dog owners. The food became so popular, it became an enterprise unto itself. Because of Mrs. Tiggywiggle's French heritage, they named their burgeoning business *Victuels pour Les Chiens*, which means "dog food" in French. Since nobody could pronounce that, they used her nickname and the company became "Frenchy's Dog Food."

Their son, Thom, who inherited the business, was a hard worker, but had little business sense. He married a woman who did, the marketing wizard named Fedelia. She took the solid local business and turned it into a global giant. She and Thom were avid dog lovers themselves and had two lap Doberman Pinschers named Perfecto and Sugar. Their son, Maxibillion, or Billy, was the current head of Frenchy's Dog Food.

"Wow! My kind of peeps," said Wags. "When's the next Woofstock?"

"This weekend," said Nomad.

"It sounds like fun!" Wags enthused.

"Not if you're a dog," said Nomad solemnly.

"But it's *for* dogs . . ."

"No, it's for *humans* who like dogs."

"What's so bad about that?"

"Well, some of the dogs have to get bathed, trimmed, brushed, and examined by humans. Others have to show how obedient they are to their humans, who make them heel, sit, down, and stay and stuff. But the worst is the agility course."

"What's that?"

"It's a whole bunch of obstacles a dog has to conquer to get a ribbon they don't care about. They have to jump over hurdles, weave through poles, crawl through tunnels, and worst of all, they have to walk the teeter-totter."

"Sounds like even more fun for me! Count me in, I'm going!"

"How're you gonna get outta here?"

"Where there's a Wags, Nomad, there's a way," said Wags firmly.

For the next week, Wags went into training in her little crate, pacing around the edges and doing push-ups. She would be ready when the time came. She didn't have a real plan, but she was confident that an opportunity would arise.

The weekend of the Frenchy's Woofstock came and almost went. It was Sunday morning, the last day, and Wags was still imprisoned at The Dogg House when Nomad came wandering into the barn.

"Where've you been?" Wags wanted to know.

"At Woofstock . . ."

"And you didn't take me?"

"How could I? You're all locked up."

"Hmmm," said Wags, going into a state of deep concentration. After a few moments, she said brightly, "I've got an idea."

"I was afraid of that," Nomad sighed, resigned to his fate as a friend of Wags.

Chapter 3

Escape!

Craig Cruikshank, Francis Cruikshank's nephew, was sitting in the office of The Dogg House at one corner of the barn. He was a husky boy with an iBook glued to his lap and his feet up on a desk. The space was just the desk, several chairs, and a few makeshift walls adorned with photos of his uncle's championship dogs wearing multicolored ribbons. Craig dreamt of having a virtual reality system and someday designing the system himself because he preferred a virtual community to the real world. He had no use for dogs, but took on the task of maintenance of The Dogg House, even though the money he made barely covered upgrades to his current system. Craig was deep into his Mineshaft video game that morning, proudly sailing up the levels of enchantment as never before.

Inside the cage marked #63, Wags was scheming with Nomad. She said to Nomad, "Here's what we'll do. That nephew of Frank's, Craig, over there in the office, is minding the store while everyone's at Woofstock, and he's slower than mud. I'll start screeching like I've been bitten by a shark. Craig'll amble over to see what's wrong. He'll reach down to open the cage to see what's up with me, and when he does, you bite him on the ankle, hard! Then I'll run out."

"I don't know. I might go to jail."

"At least you'll get fed there."

"No, I don't think s—"

"Too late now!" Wags began screeching like she'd been bitten by a shark.

. . .

Craig was oblivious of nearly everything but his game until Wags's earsplitting yelps transcended the normal clamor of The Dogg House and pierced his concentration. He kept going, thinking that maybe the infuriating dog would get over it. As he continued to navigate the challenges of his game, her squeals got louder. He knew his uncle would have a fit if something happened to one of the dogs, so he resentfully slammed his laptop shut and stalked over to the cage marked #63. "Whassa matta wit' you?" he said, cracking the door open.

Nomad, who had slunk back into the nether reaches of the barn, dashed out and sunk his teeth into the boy's ankle.

Craig shrieked and stumbled backwards. Wags wriggled her way out of the cage and ran. Nomad took off as fast as he'd arrived. Wags leapt with joy. It was her first step toward becoming a Tiggywiggle! She shot through the door of the barn like a bullet, leaving Craig dazed by Nomad's attack and her escape.

"Whaaaat?" he gasped. "Where'd they go?" The dog who'd bitten him had torn his trousers but hadn't drawn blood. Still, Craig was furious as he scanned the area for the culprits. There were no loose dogs in sight. The cage door was ajar, and the space was empty. All the residents of The Dogg House were screeching. Craig's head was spinning. He would be in deeper doo-doo with Uncle Francis than the dogs.

Bursting with joy, Wags tore around in circles and figures of eight out in the barnyard, never once looking back. Her circles grew wider and wider. As she raced through the kitchen gardens, tiny cherry tomatoes and wisps of dill weed lodged in her fur. She frolicked in the pickle patch. Then she made a game of wriggling in and out of rows of late-summer corn, collecting its silk as she bounded forward. The joy of the moment overtook her mission until she flopped down on the ground at the entrance to the woods to catch her breath. The cherry tomatoes rolled off of her into the dust. Then, reality took hold.

She was still at Fagin's Resort and still hungry. Craig had been too busy with his game to remember to feed and water the dogs. As he had climbed through the levels of his game, the thought of his duty receded. He'd get to it before his uncle returned, hefigured, but promptly forgot.

Wags had no experience in the wild and therefore had no idea of where to go or how to fill her empty void. As she looked around her, the answer came slinking out of the bushes.

"Follow me," Nomad instructed her. And she did.

He guided her into the woods between Fagin's Resort and The Wishing Well. There were many chaseable creatures, but Wags and Nomad ignored them and forged on through the foliage. Chipmunks and squirrels skittered out of their way, doves cooed, finches sang, woodpeckers tapped their trees, and bigger animals lurked out of sight. Running through the brush, Wags and Nomad collected all manner of plant matter in their coats. When they came out of the woods on the other side, they were almost completely camouflaged, looking more like miniature forested hills than dogs.

"Now what?" Wags asked as they came to a stop before the broad, grassy prairie of Brambles' Sward.

"To Frenchy's Woofstock. It's just over that hillock to the east at The Wishing Well, and once we're at the fair, there's food for all."

"And what about the Tiggywiggles?"

"You'll see. It's their shindig, so they'll all be there."

"What'cha waiting for?" Wags responded, running forward, leaving Nomad in her wake.

Chapter 4

Frenchy's Woofstock

Like Kind Kirby had said, The Wishing Well estate was not far away in distance, but worlds beyond the seediness of The Dogg House. Each year, on the third weekend of August, Frenchy's Dog Food sponsored a massive dog jamboree on the property. It was a weekend of frivolity for dogs and their humans that benefitted causes for a variety of animals, including the Doggo-Rama Sanctuary, Cataholics Anonymous, and the American Society of Pizza for Captive Animals (ASPizzaCA). What started several decades ago as a company picnic had grown into a major destination for dog lovers.

The festival grounds encircled the house like a moat, so there was no escaping it for denizens of The Wishing Well. This was a problem for Maxibillion X. (Billy) Tiggy-wiggle, the current President of Frenchy's Dog Food, who was not a fan of the event. He resented dogs in general because he felt the family dogs had been treated better than he was when he was a child. Most often, he'd slink off to Lake Lucy for some bird-watching after opening the festival with short speeches crediting the sponsors and the causes they supported. This year, his parents Thom and Fedelia, who normally regaled the crowds, were out of town to help shepherd dogs who were homeless from a tornado in Kansas. As company president, Billy was expected to be at the festival. With his parents gone, he couldn't sneak away. More importantly, his children loved Woofstock since Billy didn't allow dogs on the property at any other time and dogs were their passion.

Billy remained firm in his resolve not to have dogs in residence at The Wishing Well, but he couldn't help savoring the joy reflected in his family during Woofstock. His family was his rapture in life. He could hardly believe his good fortune in finding his extraordinary wife, Hortense, and building their happy family together. Every day, he luxuriated in the love he'd longed for as a child. Now, he had more love than he could ever have imagined with his wife and their two children Beatrix (Bea) and Augustus (Auggie).

. . .

Wags and Nomad stopped to assess the situation. Standing atop a high esker formed by glaciers millennia ago, they could see a house that looked like a flying saucer planted in the prairie in the distance. Between them and the house was an open savannah known as Brambles' Sward. Native plants and buzzing bees thrived there. Abundant milkweed pods were ready to burst, releasing their seed to the wind. Black-eyed Susans and purple coneflowers created a cheerful cacophony of color ornamented with butterflies swarming in that rich habitat for myriad creatures.

A broad roof arched over glassed-in galleries of rooms of the home, blending nature and interior seamlessly. The foundation of local Lannon stone from a nearby quarry united the house with its surroundings. On one end, the glass extended into a vaulted greenhouse with wing-like windows that opened upward toward the sun in warmer weather. Sioux Creek babbled its way around the building with gentle, constant motion. Toward the back of the house was an amoeba-shaped swimming pool and a bank of garages filled with energy-efficient cars and an assortment of bikes and skateboards. An old stone well with a wooden roof, the property's namesake, was prominently positioned in front of the house.

Sioux Creek meandered through the property, spreading out into a small lagoon, Lake Lucy, to the east of the house. Small wooden bridges over the river connected pathways through the prairie and the woods to the west. Elegant, long-legged blue herons liked to stop among the tall brush and cattails along the Sioux.

The fairgrounds were alive with dogs and people. For Woofstock, areas of the prairie had been cleared for sporting activities, booths, and parking. In the agility ring, a variety of obstacles, like the ones Nomad had described to Wags, were set up. The Rally Obedience course had a dozen stations with signs indicating which obedience skills the competitors had to demonstrate at each stop, like sit, stand, and walk back three steps. There were separate areas for Conformation and Non-Conformation (the mixed breed competition), Stunt Dog competitions, and Wheelchair Mushing. Some dogs were leaping into the pool. Others were chasing mechanical lures on a large course set up on the turf and generally having great fun.

Wags and Nomad sprinted over to the fairgrounds and huddled together behind stacked cases of Frenchy's Dog Food. From their hiding spot, they observed an arrogant-looking Afghan Hound standing calmly on a grooming table as several humans brushed out his long locks and trimmed his nails. The Au Naturel Pet Store's exhibit booth was chock-full of wonderments for dogs that Wags had never even imagined. Under one of the tables, a belligerent Beagle argued fiercely with a toy alien. Looking like moving mounds of yard refuse, Wags and Nomad began exploring the grounds as stealthily as possible.

In one area, a couple dozen dogs in various attire were being judged for the best costume. The winner appeared to be a dog dressed up like a Chia Pet. None of the dog herself was visible beneath the lush growth of little faux leaves that covered her entire body. Other contenders included a small dog in an alligator costume who was quite fearsome-looking and a gigantic lady Leonberger in a pink tutu.

In a tent painted to look like a mini castle, Sir Uther, pet psychic, sat upon an impressive golden throne wearing a sorcerer's pointed hat and a long purple cape with white fur trim. Sir Uther had a large dog draped across his lap. Seemingly impervious to the discomfort of his regal garments in the summertime heat, Sir Uther lightly stroked the dog's back as he talked seriously with a human hovering closely to hear his findings. "He sees himself as an English gentleman who likes to smoke cigars," he said to her. "Oh dear," she said. "We don't allow smoking on our property!" Then she asked him if her dog was unhappy because he liked to run away whenever he got a chance. "Oh no," said Sir Uther, "he just has a great sense of adventure." A long line of dogs and humans waited in line for their chance to consult the oracle.

Nomad and Wags paused at the Non-Conformation contest. All manner of canines and humans were gathered in a large circle. Several humans with clipboards were closely evaluating the contestants, which included a large dog with a copper-colored head, white body sprinkled with subtle spots, and a long, wagging tail. There was a medium-sized entrant that looked like a dirty mop with so much fur that it was hard to distinguish head from tail except for its beady, black eyes and

shiny snout. A low-to-the ground dog with short fur, a long nose, a bushy tail, and pointy ears was rolling on his back with great enthusiasm.

"Where are the Tiggywiggles?" Wags was puzzled because the humans looked all alike to her.

"They're over yonder on the other side of the agility course at the food tent."

A sign over the tent read: "Victuels pour Les Personnes (People Food)" Smoke was rising from the grills, and long tables were laden with food. Toothless Walter Wysywyg, Billy Tiggywiggle's father-in-law, was playing "Hound Dog" on guitar with his band, Extortionist Love Puppy. Big Mama Wysywyg, a slender woman with a bodacious voice, was wailing on vocals with Felonius Hunk, the Wysywyg's pure-white Bulldog, plunking out the melody on the piano.

The Tiggywiggles were on the dance floor, laughing and singing along with Big Mama Wysywyg. Billy, a tall, slender man with a blond mop of hair flopped over his forehead, was dancing with his treasured daughter, Bea, a lovely girl with masses of shiny black curls spiraling in all directions from her head and a dazzling white smile. Hugging her tightly, they were head-to-head as her father twirled her around with her legs spinning out in the wind.

Billy's wife, Hortense, was a beautiful woman with a lush figure, the same hair as Bea, and the same freckled nose and cheeks as their son, Auggie. Auggie's longish, fuzzy, dark hair with golden highlights fell over his forehead like his dad's.

Wags had never seen people laugh before, but she knew happiness when she saw it and hungered for that as much as she did for food.

"We'll get caught if we stay out here in the open," Nomad warned.

"That's exactly what I'm hoping for!"

"Not if Cranky Franky finds you. He'll take you right back to The Dogg House. He and that scrawny wife of his are around here somewhere. They sponsor the art show. Let's go hide under the stands at the agility course and get the lay of the land before we make any quick moves."

"OK," said Wags, a little disappointed that she couldn't just instantaneously become a Tiggywiggle.

The agility ring was in a large fenced-in area with a bank of stands on one side. The course of obstacles was set up inside it, including hurdles, tunnels, a dozen vertical poles in a line, a hoop dangling from a large framework, a long, high plank, a steep A-frame ramp, and the dreaded teeter-totter. Nomad and Wags approached carefully and hunkered down below the stands where they could see what was going on in the ring without being detected.

When they arrived, Monty, a large Bernese Mountain Dog, was lumbering around the course lackadaisically. He was clearly not interested in the sport. His human, Finessa Bopp, the chef/owner of the Dandy Diner, trotted enthusiastically alongside of him, indicating with verbal cues the obstacles she wanted him to do.

"Dog walk!" she called out to him.

Monty strode up the steep ramp to the high plank, traversed it slowly, and then exited on the other side. With a word from Bopp, he hopped through the hoop jump that was barely big enough for his girth. From there, she guided him to the weave poles. He halfheartedly walked in and out of them. Monty loved Finessa and was willing to cooperate with her game plans to a point. When she waved him over to a large teeter-totter, he came to a halt at the end of it.

"Teeter!" said Bopp brightly. Monty turned his head toward her and gave her the stink eye.

"Oh, c'mon, Monty!" Bopp implored. When Monty began to lift his leg on the teeter-totter in protest, she cried out, "No! No! No!"

An official with an ID badge hanging from a lanyard looked at a sheet on his clipboard and said firmly, "Disqualified!"

"But he didn't do anything!" said Bopp.

"Precisely. Disqualified!" said the judge curtly.

Finessa Bopp said nothing more. Dejectedly, she hooked Monty onto a lead and headed off the course with her head down in disgrace and disappointment. Monty, looking satisfied with himself, ambled amiably by her side.

"I could do that," Wags whispered to Nomad. They stayed and watched more competitors of various breeds and abilities. Wags observed the strengths and failings of each competitor, convinced she could outdo them all. She wasn't scared of the steep A-frame, the high dog walk, or the teeter-totter. It all looked like the best of fun to her.

Over at the Victuels pour Les Personnes tent, the Tiggywiggles were now loading their plates with grilled goodies. Mrs. Hortense Tiggywiggle had a mountain of salad on her plate. Bea and Auggie were decorating their hamburgers with ketchup and mustard faces.

"Nice!" said Auggie to his sister, noting the ketchup frown and a wiggle of mayo for hair on her burger.

"It's Cranky Franky," Beatrix whispered, laughing.

"Shhhh," Auggie warned, but couldn't suppress a giggle. Bea joined in the laughter, and he said, "Bea, I don't like him either, but . . ."

"Uh-oh. He's right over there!" Bea took her plastic knife and smeared the ketchup frown and mayo hair away.

Billy Tiggywiggle was just about to bite into his luscious Beach Burger when Francis Cruikshank and his wife, Cookie, walked by.

"Cranky . . . er, Francis, Cookie," Billy greeted.

"Hmm," Francis grumbled.

"What've you got there, Billy?" Cookie asked.

"Oh." Billy was relieved to have something noncontroversial to talk about. "It's my Beach Burger."

Cookie Cruikshank raised one eyebrow in question.

"It's quite delicious!" Billy enthused. "It's a thick, savory lentil patty with grilled onions, slices of avocado, and a dab of mayo on one of Ms. Bopp's homemade buns."

"Humph," Francis sniffed.

"Well, to each their own," Cookie said, grabbing her husband by the arm and moving away from the Tiggywiggles toward the festival marketplace. "Eh," he grunted in agreement, turning his back on the host family and trudging off.

Cookie and Francis were two of Endwell's elites, or at least they liked to think so. As the owners of Fagin's Cars for the Stars, they were well known to everyone. Like a queen indulging the peasants with her presence, Cookie greeted all in passing with a nod here and there while her husband was silently regal in attitude, though somewhat shabby-looking. The original Amazin' Fagin was Cookie's father, Fast Eddie Fagin. She'd taken over the business after her father passed on to the Cadillac in the sky. She brought Francis into the business when they married. Cookie was the face of the business, as she had been from childhood in their TV and radio commercials. She was beloved by many from afar, but for those who knew her well, let's just say some of them felt differently.

Hortense, barely suppressing giggles as she watched the couple parade past them, said to her husband, "Have you ever seen Cookie eat anything more than a leaf of lettuce?"

The children sputtered laughter through their lips.

"Shush, kids, it's not nice to laugh," their mother scolded.

"Cookie? Er, yes, of course, on occasion she'll have a nibble . . . and not to be snarky, but what's that pile of rabbit food doing on your plate?" Billy asked with a smile. He was raised on what he considered rabbit food because he was chubby as a child. He always felt that the family dogs ate better than he did, and that's why he hated dogs. Unfortunately, or fortunately for him, he made a fortune feeding dogs and was obligated to sponsor Woofstock every year.

"Honeyacre Farms provided all the veggies for the salad bar, dearest. I'm not dieting, I couldn't resist. It's a magnificent buffet. They brought all their produce to Woofstock, so they had to leave a sign on their empty garden stand that says, 'For veggies, go to Woofstock.' That heap of onions on your burger is their signature honeybunions."

"Delicious," Billy muffled with his mouth full of Beach Burger.

The family ate their meals amiably, talking in between mouthfuls. When their plates were almost empty, Hortense said, "Let's eat up, children. I'd like to go see the agility competition. I hear Mrs. Ardmore's Dalmatian, Pollock, is a sight to see."

"I like Wendy Willow's Greyhound. She's fast as lightning," Auggie enthused.

"And don't forget Mr. Gypsum's Pomeranian, Gypsy!" Bea jumped into the conversation.

Auggie's expression turned serious as he faced his dad.

"Dadoid, why can't we have a dog? We don't care what kind, shape, or size. Bea and I'll feed him, take him for walks, groom him, and do anything else he needs."

"Yeah," said Bea, supporting her brother.

Billy, mouth full, chewing his burger, couldn't speak, but shook his head firmly "no."

"Momzella, we already have a name picked out, and we'd like to take her to the agility class at the Endwell Kennel Club," said Bea, addressing her mom.

"Dadoid, er, your father, has spoken, and his answer is no."

"But Momzella, you want a dog too, don't you?" Bea insisted.

"Let's go see the agility trials," said Hortense, avoiding the question. "Billy, you can join us when you're finished. It'll be fun!" Hortense and the kids deposited their paper plates in the recycling bin and headed off.

"Funph?" Billy said to no one with his mouth full of Beach Burger.

Along the way to the agility competition, Auggie bounced up and down, pestering his mom about a dog. "Guess what we're gonna call him?"

Hortense did not respond. Getting into this topic could get her into trouble since he was right: she too longed for a dog.

"Milagro!" Bea said excitedly. "We learned it in Spanish class. It means 'miracle.'"

"'Cause it'd be a miracle if we got one," Auggie added.

"And Luz, which means 'light,' if it's a girl because she would be the light of our lives," said Bea.

They found seats in the middle of the stands where they had a good view of the whole course.

"Oh, there's Mrs. Ardmore's Pollock coming onto the course," said Hortense, changing the subject. "We're just in time!"

Billy Tiggywiggle lagged behind his family, swallowing the last of his burger as he plodded over to the agility ring. With so many interruptions, he hadn't had a chance to really enjoy his favorite meal. Being at Woofstock kept bringing back wretched memories of his childhood. His mother, Fedelia, a good soul at heart, had worried that he'd suffer bullying as a pudgy little boy. She also secretly feared that he'd grow up to be a wooly mammoth like his grandfather, Whiskers, the butcher who launched the family's dog food company.

Thus, she fed her son mostly salads and veggies. When she got wind of the presumed benefits of Chittenango Boma, a tea allegedly made by Australian aboriginals for weight control, she made Billy choke down the vile liquid with every meal. (There was no research indicating that Australian aboriginals or their children were chubby and needed weight reduction teas.)

Billy felt that his mother's lap Doberman Pinschers, Perfecto and Sugar, ate better than he did. Their dog food looked like a major improvement over anything that appeared on his plate every day. He also resented them for all the praise heaped upon them for doing nothing more than breathing. Billy's parents were so possessed by their dogs, they barely noticed his own many achievements like archery and beekeeping.

Billy dejectedly plopped down on the end of a riser at the far side of the field, where he could stew semi-privately in his own juices.

On the course, Mrs. Ardmore waited for the judge to start their run. The instant the judge gave the signal, Pollock bolted toward the first obstacle. As expected, the snow-white Hound liberally splattered with ink-black spots took the course at lightning speed. It was as if he had known the course and had been practicing it for months. Mrs. Ardmore simply tilted her head slightly this way and that to indicate the next obstacle. Pollock loved agility. He sailed effortlessly over the jumps and maneuvered each challenge with zest. He shot through the hanging hoop, dashed through the weaves without missing a pole, and took the tall dog walk like it was a launching pad. Coming down on the end ramp, he looked like he was dangling from a parachute from high altitude.

"Wow! He's lit!" Auggie said in wonder.

"Go Pollock!" Bea called out.

"That looks like such fun," Hortense mused to no one but herself.

"I could watch this for hours," said Auggie.

"I'd like to do it with our own dog for days!" Bea said.

Next up was Mr. Armstrong's chunky black Pug, Louie, who was surprisingly agile. With slow, rhythmic timing, he hefted his rather thick form over and through each task. At the end, he and his human trotted proudly off the course.

Irene Baker's happy-go-lucky, apricot-colored Labradoodle, Harry the Hodag, provided comic relief, sauntering around the field at his own variable pace. Lackadaisically he wandered in and out of the weave poles, then he picked up speed and raced over the A-frame with such enthusiasm, he landed all catawampus on his hind end with his legs askew in all directions.

"Oh, Harry, you old Hodag," Ms. Baker lamented with amusement and ill-placed pride. "Come here." Ms. Baker managed to corral Harry, put him on a leash, and give him a treat. In truth, Harry did not resemble a Rhinelander Hodag, which was described by residents of the Northern Wisconsin hamlet, where it was known to make appearances, as a mythical creature with the head of a frog, the grinning face of a giant elephant, thick, short legs, feet with huge claws, the back of a dinosaur, and a long tail with spears at the end. Harry, though not truly a Hodag, was unique in his own way.

Harry was the last contestant. The judge was determining the winners and organizing the ribbon ceremony when a tiny ball of fluff mired with plant debris burst onto the course.

"Wha—?" the audience seemed to expel together in awe.

Without a human guide, Wags took to the course with cool self-assurance. Auggie, who'd been timing each trial, punched his iWatch to start as Wags whizzed by. She tackled every obstacle in the proper order at warp speed.

The judge turned around at the commotion and stood silent in puzzlement and amazement. Who could this little dog be, and who did she/he belong to?

Wags finished the course and took a victory lap around the ring. The crowd laughed, cheered, and clapped their approval.

"He won, he won, he won!" Auggie shouted to the judge.

"He? How do you know she's a he?" Bea said, miffed.

"Who cares?" said Auggie. "He/she won. And without anyone to guide him, er, her! Mr. Arbuthnot," he said to the judge, "are you gonna give him the ribbon?"

"Hardly. He's not entered," replied the judge.

With an "I'll show you" attitude, Wags charged up the teeter-totter once again, this time with such energy that she flew off the end, catapulting herself into the air. She seemed to be suspended in midair for an instant before landing right in Billy Tiggy-wiggle's lap.

"What? Ugh! Yuck-o! A dog! In my lap!"

he gasped, lurching upward and brushing the nuisance away.

Before he could say another word, Wags dashed away. Bea and Auggie took off from their places in the stands in hot pursuit of the little stray dog.

Hortense walked over to her husband, who was deeply shaken by the dog's unexpected arrival in his lap. She put her arm around his shoulders and said, "She picked you, dearie!"

"Well, I didn't pick her!"

"If the kids catch up with her, the least we can do is give her shelter until we can find her family."

"No way!"

"Way, dear heart. We'll keep her out of *your* way. It's what the kids have always wanted."

"We give them everything," he whined.

"Everything but a dog, sweet Billy, and now she's arrived."

Chapter 5

Wags Wiggles Her Way Into The Wishing Well

Wags let the kids catch up with her and levitated herself into Bea's arms as Bea reached down to catch her. Then she leapt over into Auggie's arms. The kids juggled her back and forth like they were passing a football. All the while, Wags was wiggling and waggling with joy. She'd found her peeps.

"I've never seen such a waggly dog," Bea giggled.

"Her whole body wags," Auggie agreed.

"That's it!"

"What?"

"Wags! That's her name!"

"That's brilliant, Bea," said Auggie. Turning to his new, temporary dog, he asked, "Wags, what do you think of your new name?"

Wags wagged her approval. After all, by chance, they'd figured out her true name. She was happier than she'd ever been. Her dream of becoming a Tiggywiggle was coming true—although the dad human was still fuming.

"What've you got there, Auggie?" inquired an older man, round in every respect, with a shock of unruly, curly white hair dashing down his forehead. His round, black glasses magnified a set of glittering brown eyes alive with merriment. He had freckles like Hortense and Auggie and a pure-white goatee. He'd been watching a team on the Wheelchair Mushing course when the kids and Wags nearly bowled him over.

"She's our new dog, Uncle Brambles," Auggie gushed. "We just named her . . ."

"Wags," Bea butted in.

"Where'd she come from?" inquired Uncle Brambles.

"She just appeared on the agility course and then shot off the teeter-totter right into Dadoid's arms!" Augie said.

"I wish you wouldn't refer to your father that way . . . by the way, he looks miserable. He couldn't have approved of you keeping her. He loathes dogs."

Hortense and Billy joined the children, their uncle, and their wiggling new dog.

"Billy, we'll just have to keep her until we find her family," Hortense said, caressing Wags's head gently.

"No!" Billy responded emphatically.

"Think of the bad publicity if people found out we'd left this darling little creature out in the cold after being abandoned at Woofstock."

"Cold? It's 89 degrees in the shade!" Billy expelled a short breath of frustration. "Phut!"

"I hope we never, ever find them," said Auggie.

"Billy Tiggywiggle with a dog! It's a wonder," Brambles chuckled.

"A *temporary* dog, Uncle Bram. Only *temporary*," Billy said firmly.

To Brambles, her uncle and treasured mentor, Hortense asked, "So, now what? The kids haven't found her owners, so, what'll we do with her now?"

Brambles pondered the question seriously, twisting his goatee with his fingers. "What to do . . . what to do? Aha! I know! Give the dog a bath!"

"Of course!" said Hortense. "Kids, you're done with your chores here at Woofstock, so let's take Wags back to the house and see if we can clean her up in the laundry tub. Then we'll go from there."

Brambles sauntered over to Billy and wrapped his arm around his shoulders. "Not to worry, old boy, she's just a little mite of a dog."

"But it's a *dog*, Bram. A *dog*. They're just no good. Already a perfectly fine day gone to the dogs. I couldn't even eat my Beach Burger in peace."

"Let me buy you a refreshing Spotted Guernsey brew, Billy, and you can tell me all about it."

Uncle Brambles guided Billy, who agreed with the wisdom of having a break, off to the food tent while Hortense followed the kids and Wags as they skipped toward the house. Wags was beaming her joy like a sun to all around her. For Hortense and the kids, Wags was a keeper. Hortense couldn't help wishing that this matted ball of fur was truly a stray so they *could* keep her. The only obstacle was Billy.

At the house, Wags jumped from Auggie's arms right into the laundry tub. She was unfamiliar with the rite of bathing, so she squirmed and growl-barked at the water coming out of the faucet and nipped at the tiny soap bubbles.

"It's OK, little Wags," Bea said comfortingly as she and Auggie stood side by side massaging soap into her fur.

Wags looked doubtful. She liked her earthy aroma and hiding under all the grass and sticks she'd collected in the woods. It all gave her a sense of security. If this is what it took to become a Tiggywiggle, however, she was all for it.

By now, she was raving with hunger, so she barked her order to Auggie.

"Food, please!" Wags barked.

"Hold on, Wags, we're almost finished," Auggie said.

Observing Wags and her happy children, Hortense's heart melted. If only Billy could enjoy this magic too, then life would be perfect.

Wags barked again, more insistently this time.

"Food!" said Bea. "I think she's hungry!"

"She's in the right place for that," Hortense said cheerily. "The biggest problem will be picking out what flavor to try first. Auggie, I'm assigning you that job. There're cases of dog food for Woofstock in the back hallway."

Auggie rushed off and moments later was back with a can of food, a spoon, and a large coffee mug.

"Chicken Liver!" he proclaimed.

"Ew," said Bea, wrinkling her nose in disgust.

Whatever, Wags thought. *Just let me at it!*

Auggie opened the can and scooped the food into the mug. Wags leapt for it and sunk her teeth into a hunk of food before the re-purposed coffee cup touched the ground. *Nirvana,* she thought.

"She seems to like it," Bea said.

"Slow down, Wags," Auggie advised.

Wags paid no attention as she dug into her scoop of fragrant Frenchy's Dog Food like she'd never eaten before. She certainly had never eaten anything this good ever in her life. She knew that life as a Tiggywiggle was for her.

When she finished, her new family thought she could use some grooming.

"The bath was easy," said Bea, wrapping Wags in a towel. "Trying to get all this junk out of her coat is another story."

"Momzella, you used to groom your Irish Setter, Shanty, didn't you?" asked Auggie.

"Yes, love, I did, and Shanty was a big girl with long, silky, red fur that got very matted. She hated grooming." Hortense looked at

Wags and said, "I've handled worse than you. I'll get all that debris out of your fur."

Wags thought she'd put up with almost anything to be a Tiggywiggle.

They all laughed with the joy of their good fortune.

Chapter 6

The DArt Competition

Back at Woofstock, Brambles tried to cheer up Billy with a refreshing, cold draft brew. The snooty Cruikshanks were perusing the vender booths. They proudly flaunted Anastasia and Vladi, their elegant white Borzois. Cookie handed the leashes to her husband so she could take a look at some merchandise at the Au Naturel Pet Store booth that was festooned with dog paraphernalia.

Holding up a large, pink fleece jacket with a fluffy, fake fur collar, she said to her husband, "Cranky . . ."

He bristled at hearing his loathed nickname.

"Grrrr," was all he said.

"What do you think of this for Ani? And maybe the brown one for Vladi."

"Hunph," Francis intoned with a smirk of reluctant agreement.

"We'll take these two," Cookie said to Faith Carmichael, the vendor. "And two bags of the duck jerky and that large tin of chicken tenders."

She turned to the dogs and said, "See, Mummy and Daddy love you!"

Addressing no one in particular, she said, "Wouldn't little Billy Tiggywiggle be jealous? He always said the dogs ate better than he did!"

Cookie and Billy had been high school sweethearts. Cookie was sweet on Billy's fortune, and he just went along with dating her because it was expected of him. Dating Cookie, his lifelong schoolmate, if not friend, was as normal as putting on his socks in the morning. Cookie thought their relationship would lead to marriage, and it would have, if Billy hadn't encountered the enchanting Hortense Wysywyg on the day before his college graduation, when he'd planned to propose to Cookie.

Billy was immediately entranced with Hortense's freckles that cheerfully danced across her nose and cheeks as she served him coffee at the Dandy Diner. Her engaging smile and voluptuous figure were mighty fine as well. Hortense's beauty, her sweet fragrance like flowers, and her kind manner made him forget his plan to propose to Cookie. Hortense and Billy blended together like coffee and cream. Their life together began lovingly in that moment.

Cookie reluctantly had to settle for second best, Francis Cruikshank, who had ardently pursued her for years. His expensive gifts, fine dining meals, and promises of trips the world over finally wore her down, and she accepted his proposal. Somehow, she managed to overlook his gruff temperament and scruffy appearance. Cocktail hour, when she could drift into a dreamy wakefulness, had become her favorite time of the day.

"Come now, Francis, children! Let's eat!"

The two Borzois were the couple's only children. Although the Cruikshanks both had close relatives nearby and enough money to lavishly support over a dozen families, in their wills, they gave everything to a fund for their dogs and the rest to the Fix Network Scholarship Fund. Not even a dime would go to Craig, who was an oaf, but an oaf who came in handy, helping out here and there, thinking he was banking brownie points with his aunt and uncle.

Francis and Cookie, with the Borzois in the lead, looked like a chariot of aristocrats, which, in their little world, they were. Cookie picked out a table in the Victuels Tent, put the dogs in a firm stay, and pulled her husband toward the food and beverages.

Shortly thereafter, their table was littered with cups and plates. Cookie put a plate laden with Beach Burgers on the ground for the dogs. She gazed ravenously at her plate of fried chicken, buttered corn on the cob, and an impressive stack of fries. Looking at the meal wistfully, she pushed it toward her husband and edged a smaller plate with a cream puff closer to herself. She picked up the delectable pastry and nibbled a couple molecules of the dreamy, creamy, sweet filling and the crispy, slightly savory puff. How she longed to devour everything on all the plates! But she stayed true to her dedication to health and fitness and left the rest behind.

"Well, it's not like dinner at the Kennelworth Country Club," Cookie said to her husband. "There aren't any of those Cannibal Sandwiches you so enjoy, dear, but we'll manage somehow." The Kennelworth was an exclusive country club where the rich didn't have to mingle with the commoners to get their dinner.

These days, Francis was on the "See Food" diet. He saw food, and he ate it. Cookie was right, though; his favorite meal was Cannibal Sandwiches, also known as Steak Tartar: open-faced sandwiches of raw, ground sirloin on thin, dark rye bread, piled high with finely diced onions, salt, freshly cracked pepper, and topped with a raw egg yolk.

The car dealer, who once had a thick, but firm, wrestler's build, now had a "Milwaukee Goiter," a beer belly that overhung his belt and strained the knit fabric of his expensive pink golf shirt. There was a greasy orange stain on his chest fringed with fragments of napkin where Cookie had attempted to clean him up. After eating his food and Cookie's, he was bloated and gassy. This was a frequent occurrence at meals. When he emanated his noxious fumes, he sloughed the blame onto the dogs, looking at them with distain as if they'd deeply offended him.

"I'm full!" Cookie announced, with the only item she'd sampled barely touched. Francis lifted the remains of her cream puff and engorged it like a snake swallowing a seemingly impossible large prey. Leaving the table and the ground around it strewn with debris, the foursome headed off toward the DArt (Dog Art) competition that they sponsored. There was no avoiding Billy and Brambles sitting at a table in their path with their heads together, nodding in blissful mirth.

"Billy. Bram," Cookie said curtly.

"Oh, hello!" Billy and Brambles said in unison.

"What are you laughing at?" Cookie demanded.

"Oh, we're not laughing *at* any*one* or any*thing*, Cookie," Brambles answered. "We're laughing *with* the universe."

"Huh!" Cookie sniffed.

"Care to join us?" Billy invited them with a wave of his cup toward two empty chairs at their table.

"Grrrruff," Francis responded shortly.

"How was your lunch?" Billy asked.

"Nothing like The Kennelworth," Cookie said disdainfully, brushing past Billy and Brambles in a huff.

Brambles and Billy sputtered, trying to suppress their giggles. When they had both reclaimed their composure, Brambles said to Billy, "It's time I get over to the DArt competition. I'm a judge. Why don't you come with me?"

"Because I hate dogs and it's just silly. Dogs

can't make art ... Dog Art. DArt. Phooey! It's ridiculous," Billy scoffed.

"Oh c'mon, it'll give you time to adjust to the idea that you'll have a dog of your own when you get home."

"Oh no you don't! Bram, we're just taking her in until we find her family . . . and the sooner the better."

"We'll see," said Brambles, walking with Billy toward the DArt booth. "I hear that Mr. Armstrong's Pug, Louie, in addition to his skill in agility, is quite a good abstract expressionist. I know you love art, Billy. You can help me pick the winners."

Brambles bustled ahead, and Billy followed reluctantly, shaking his head in disbelief. Finessa Bopp was now directing activities at the DArt area. Monty, after his agility debacle, was sleeping in a large dog bed, snoring contentedly. Several young people under Finessa's direction were helping by squeezing the paints on canvases and then covering them with thick, clear plastic bags for the dog artists to tread on, making their unique works of art.

"Louie really likes that China blue with pale yellow and Prussian blue accents," Mr. Armstrong said to Bopp.

"Here are the colors, Patience," Finessa said to one of the girls, handing her three tubes of paint. "But just a gnat's eyelash of the darker blue . . . A little goes a long way, and Louie's very particular about his color choices."

Patience giggled softly, preparing the canvas and setting it on the ground for the Pug and his proud papa. "Hey, Louie, come here," she said, luring him with a dog cookie.

Louie sniffed around the edges of the paint-loaded canvas covered with plastic wrap. He looked up at his owner, who was beaming. Mr. Armstrong greeted Brambles and Billy with joy. "Ah, Mr. Wysywyg and Mr. Tiggywiggle. Here's an old master in the making. Just watch him. Last year, Louie's piece took third place. He's going for a win this year."

"It's just Brambles and Billy, Mr. Armstrong. I was just telling Billy about Louie's artistic abilities," Brambles said.

Louie walked slowly around the odd object on the ground, nudging it doubtfully here and there with his snout. Then he walked a safe distance away from it, plopped down on his belly, and shot his hind legs out like a frog.

"Louie!" said Mr. Armstrong, trying to get his dog's attention. But Louie flopped over on his side and started to snore loudly. Then Mr. Armstrong tried to lure Louie over to the canvas with another treat. "Dried Kunstler's liver sausage. Your favorite." Louie lifted his head to gaze at his owner momentarily and then, immobilized with exhaustion, went back to sleep.

"Billy, I think he needs a little help," said Brambles.

"Don't look at me. I'm just here for the art."

Brambles took Louie's lead and handed it to Billy.

"No way!"

"Way. I can't help. I'm a judge. Here!" Brambles said, scooping up the chunky Pug and shoving him into Billy's arms.

Billy treated Louie like a hot potato, quickly depositing him on the plastic-wrapped canvas. Louie acted like the canvas was hot coals and danced off it in a flash. Patience immediately came back over, carefully removed the plastic from the canvas, and put it on a drying table.

"You see what I mean, Billy?" said Brambles, looking at the drying work of art. "Not to be partial to any one contestant, but you can see that Louie is gifted at abstracts. I have the dickens of a time with abstracts myself. That's why I stick with dog sculptures," Brambles admitted.

Brambles lived in a lodge on the Tiggy-wiggle estate. Since Billy welcomed him, but didn't allow dogs on the property except during Woofstock, Brambles, a great dog lover, had taken up making sculptures of dogs that now littered every inch of his home and garden. Brambles was kind, and not at all prickly, as his name might suggest. He got the nickname because as a child, he spent much of his time scampering around the woods gathering refuse from shrubs and vines, sometimes even strands of blackberries or wild roses, in his wooly hair. He was always covered in brambles, so he became known as "Brambles" to his family, and the name stuck.

"But you are a brilliant dog sculptor, Mr.... er, Brambles," said Mr. Armstrong. "Louie and I greatly enjoyed your sculpture garden this morning, especially the Pugs, of course."

"Concrete. They'll last forever," Brambles said, beaming with pride.

"Doggone it!" Billy exclaimed. "We're all going to the dogs!"

Chapter 7

From Crusty & Dusty
to Sleek & Unique

At the house, Hortense was gently working the last of the twigs out of Wags's fur with her own hair comb, since there were no dog supplies around the house other than dog food.

"Sorry to pull on your fur, Wags, but what a good girl you are!" Turning to the kids, she said, "It's amazing that she didn't struggle more. Just a couple grumbles and grunts, otherwise smooth sailing. She still has some dreadlocks here and there. Bea, go get the scissors."

"But they're so cute on her! Just leave 'em!" Auggie implored.

"Yeah," Bea chimed in.

"OK, kids, I guess Wags will be our *dread* dog," their mother responded.

"Our dog. That has a nice ring to it," said Bea wistfully. "I hope we never find her family!"

"I hope she doesn't have a family! Except us, of course," said Auggie ardently.

"Well, kids, her real family will want her back, don't you think?"

"We *are* her real family!" the kids said in unison.

"Her people may still be somewhere on the grounds. We don't have a leash for Wags, so she'll have to stay here. Take some pictures of her with your phones and go show them around."

"Aw, Momzella," Auggie objected.

"OK," Bea reluctantly agreed.

"But stay away from Mr. Cruikshank. He's been on a smile fast his whole life, and he's meaner than a wet hen," Hortense warned. When they were growing up, he had kicked Hortense's dog, Shanty, when he thought that Hortense hadn't paid enough attention to him. She hadn't forgotten the incident.

Bea and Auggie took pictures of Wags from all angles. They'd snapped a couple of before-grooming shots as well. Then they walked back to the fairgrounds as slowly as they could while still moving. Reluctantly, they approached Woofstock-goers with their post-grooming pictures. A couple of folks thought they'd seen a dog like her, only scruffier, on the agility course, but no one claimed her. The kids' mood lifted as more and more people said that they didn't recognize Wags. After they'd covered most of the area, they went looking for their dad.

"There he is!" said Auggie.

Billy and Brambles were still at the DArt tent.

Holding up Louie Armstrong's painting, Billy said, "You know, Brambles, it's really quite good. Not exactly like the famous abstract artists, Frankenthaler or Basquiat, but it has vigor and style. Would you be interested in selling it to me, Mr. Armstrong?"

"Oh, no, Mr. Tig . . . er, Billy. It would hurt Louie's feelings, and I've got just the place for it. I'll put it next to the one he made last year."

"Well, it's a winner. It truly is."

"And this year the judges thought so too," said Mr. Armstrong, taking the picture with a blue ribbon hanging across it from Billy.

The Cruikshanks huffed away from the DArt tent just as the kids arrived. The gruesome twosome were too busy grumbling about their losses to notice anything else. Cookie held Ani's red, pink, and orange painting that had a respectable second-place ribbon on it, but Cookie felt it deserved better, especially since their car dealership sponsored the booth. Agility champion Pollock had taken third place with a speckled mess that looked like he'd chewed on tubes of paint and spit them out on the canvas—which was exactly the case. He'd stolen the paints when Patience wasn't looking. Vladi Cruikshank had submitted a dark smear of muddled blacks, browns, and greens that didn't place in the award ceremony. His proud owner, Francis, looked at it admiringly as he strode away with Cookie, burdened with dogs and purchases.

The Tiggywiggles and Brambles huddled with the prize-winning Pug, Louie.

"Wow, Louie's quite an artist," Bea enthused, coming up next to her dad. "Hey, Dadoid!"

"Hi, honey bunches of groats! Where's your mom and, er, the dog . . . ?"

"Back at the house. We named her Wags, and she looks terrific," said Auggie. "Wait'll you see her! We bathed her and then Momzella brushed her out."

"She still has some dreadlocks here and there . . . very fashionable. We're calling her our *dread* dog," said Bea.

"So, you've already got a name for her?" Brambles joined in the conversation.

"She's our animal angel, Uncle Brambles," Bea said brightly, handing Brambles her phone with the pictures of Wags.

"It's true, she *is* a fine specimen," Brambles observed, flicking through the images on her phone. "A fine specimen indeed. And she cleaned up nicely."

"Momzella made us take her picture and go see if we could find her family, but we couldn't. Nobody's claimed her," said Bea.

"You haven't seen her, have you?" Auggie asked Mr. Armstrong.

"I think I may have. Is that the dog who aced the agility course and landed in your lap, Billy?" said Mr. Armstrong, turning toward him.

"The same," said Billy. "Do you know who she belongs to?" Mr. Armstrong shook his head, and Billy's brow furrowed in a frustrated frown. "We need to get her back to her family pronto. They'll be worried sick."

"Dadoid, we talked to everyone we could find, but nobody knows her. Can we keep her? Please, can we keep her?" Auggie was just short of whining.

"You know the rules, young'uns. No dogs. We're firm on that, your mom and I. This is just temporary. She'll have to stay in the family room. Don't let her sit on my chair. I'll have to read in the living room during her *short* stay. She *won't* have the run of the house! Got that?"

"Yeah, Dadoid," Bea and Auggie said sullenly in unison. "Got it."

"All's not lost," Billy said to his beloved children. "You're doing the right thing and deserve a treat. I bet there's still some frozen custard at the Victuels tent. How about I treat you to banana splits?"

The kids were still disappointed, but the thought of a frozen custard sundae with bananas and whipped cream, topped with cherries and toasted pecans, lightened their load.

. . .

Back at the house, Hortense snuggled with a slightly damp, but warm Wags on the davenport in the living room. Wags collapsed in her new mother's arms, exhausted from the day's activities.

"Dear little one. I pray you'll stay here with us. After all, where there's a will, there's a way. Wags, we'll make it happen. We've just got to. How could I ever let you go now?"

Wags lifted her head and softly kissed Hortense on her cheek. *This is what bliss is,* Hortense thought. Wags was thinking the same thing.

Chapter 8

The Search

Frenchy's Woofstock was winding to a close. Most of the people and dogs had gone home. A few vendors were packing up, and workers were dismantling activity courses. The Tiggywiggles and Uncle Brambles were helping pick up the trash as they meandered back to the house.

The Cruikshanks had packed up their dogs, their artwork, and Cookie's many purchases in their elegant, black SUV and drove the short distance back to Fagin's Resort, Cookie's family estate. Francis was exhausted, so he planned to go right to bed. Cookie was tired too, though she'd never admit it. She was looking forward to sorting out all the merch she'd purchased and finding places for the new items in their home that was already crowded with all the stuff she'd collected.

Francis pulled the car into the garage, parked, and let Vladi out of the back. He left his door open for Cookie to close. He didn't even think about helping her unload Ani and all her purchases. Then he headed toward the barn with Vladi at his heels to check on his menagerie. Francis and Vladi, who was almost as mean and unforgiving as his owner, were inseparable.

Entering the makeshift office in the barn, Francis found Craig sitting back in a chair with his legs on the desk and his laptop propped on his thighs. The boy's fingers whizzed across the keyboard. His earbuds were pumping out the heavy metal sounds of Extortionist Love Puppy. He was far too absorbed in his own virtual world to notice his uncle.

Francis cleared his throat to get the lazy kid's attention. When that didn't work after several attempts, he nodded to Vladi, who, on command, began to bark and snarl at the boy. Their presence finally got Craig's attention. "Criminy!" he gasped, looking into the fearsome grill of his uncle's dog. "Everything's fine here. I just gotta feed the dogs," he said nervously.

Francis raised his eyebrows in question. His lips were flatlined.

"Dang! What?" Craig said with impatience. "I was just about to make level 14."

Francis's eyes grew wider, sensing something fishy in his nephew's response.

"OK, OK, Uncle Frank. No problems, really. Nothing serious."

Francis's brow furrowed, his lips curled downward, and he leaned forward and waited for his knucklehead nephew, Craig, to tell the rest of the story.

"Well, there *was* one little thing," Craig stammered. "Nothing major, really, I looked everywhere, no big loss . . . you see, this little dog escaped . . ."

Francis's cheeks puffed up like a blowfish,

and he expelled a tornadic breath through trembling lips. Craig thought he could see steam jettisoning from his uncle's ears. Francis stalked at a clipped rate to the cages of the barking dogs. As Craig jumped to attention in abject fear of his angry uncle, his treasured laptop crashed to the floor. "Noooo!" he cried, reluctantly turning away to follow his uncle to the scene of the crime.

"It's just that this little dog was screeching so loudly, it broke my concentration, so I went over and opened the cage to see what the problem was. Then, a coyote, I think it was a coyote, came out of nowhere and bit me, and that nasty little dog escaped!"

As Francis stood gaping at the open door of Wags's cage, #63, his fists closed and fury engulfed him. He was not the least concerned that his nephew might have been bitten by a rabid animal. Vladi emanated a low, menacing growl.

"That coyote, dog, or whatever, bit me!" Craig said indignantly, unrealistically expecting sympathy from his uncle. "Not to worry, though," he added bravely, "my jeans are shredded, but he didn't break my skin. No big loss, just one little dog, and you have so many! Besides that, my laptop just got smashed!"

Francis swatted angrily at Craig, missing the boy's nose by a gnat's eyelash. He turned his back and marched to the house with Vladi in tow. He entered and slammed the door so hard, it splintered the hinges. Craig pushed the ruined door open and rushed in after him, begging forgiveness. After all, he needed the money his uncle had promised him now more than ever to replace his broken laptop.

Cookie was in the living room, fitting a diamond-encrusted collar on Ani and admiring her proudly, when she heard the door slam, the angry voice of her husband, and the shrill cry of Craig's appeal for understanding. Fearing that a physical fight might erupt, she jumped up and hurried toward the voices.

Francis, breathing as hard as a steam engine, was vigorously berating his nephew.

"Holy smokes! What's wrong?" Cookie

was used to her husband's disagreeable ways, but this was over the top even for him. Eyes narrowed and shoulders shrugged in rage, he pointed toward The Dogg House.

Craig said, "It's that empty cage he's angry about. One of the dogs got out."

Cookie gasped as she drew in her breath. "Better not be #63 or you're cooked, Craig Cruikshank!" With Craig trailing behind her, she dashed out of the house beyond the garages and gardens to The Dogg House, where she discovered Wags's cage with the door cracked open and empty. She turned to Craig. "You better go help your uncle find her!" she ordered.

"What about my $50?" Craig whined.

"What about it? That's our champion dog you let out! If you don't find her, you're done! Your uncle's in the garage. Now get in the car with him and *go*. Just *go*."

As Cookie watched, Craig hustled back into the office, grabbed his broken laptop off the floor, and slipped it into his backpack. With Cookie at his heels girding him along, he trudged to the garage. Francis and Vladi were in Francis's menacing, black lowrider with flames emblazoned on its long fins. The loud engine was rumbling as the boy slinked into the passenger side of his uncle's ride. "Dumb mutt!" he hissed under his breath for fear of rousing even more fury in his uncle.

"I heard that, young man," Cookie said. "That dog is set to mate with Champion Sir Lancelot Lickalot of Lake Lucy on Saturday morning, and it's up to you to find her and make sure she's here for her date!"

In the low-slung '57 Chevy Bel Air, Francis, Craig, and Vladi crawled out of the garage. Francis bunny-hopped his sedan to shake up his ditzy nephew. Craig felt nauseous lurching up and down in his seat, but he did as he was told and scanned every direction to find #63. Finding blame everywhere but in himself, Craig felt it was the dog's fault that his laptop was broken. *She'd* be sorry when they found her, he thought to himself. He was just smart enough not to say it out loud.

. . .

At The Wishing Well, twilight descended on the prairie. A crescent moon shone, and faint stars in the sky began to glitter. On the ground, the air was slightly thick with humidity as nocturnal fireflies lit up to attract their mates. Occasionally, a fish jumping in the lake beyond the house rumpled the waters that twinkled like diamonds in the slanting shafts of light. Night birds squawked their presence.

Hortense settled her husband into a comfortable chair in the screened-in porch, and they toasted each other with glasses of their favorite white wine.

Wags, Brambles, and the children were gathered on the steps outside to play Starlight, Moonlight. While Bea turned her back, Brambles and Auggie, who were playing the ghosts, scrambled to hiding places in the shadows of the garage. Bea gently gathered a handful of slow-moving lightning bugs in her hands and then gradually opened her fingers to free the little insects that glowed on and off. Then she picked up Wags and sat on the back stairs as she recited the incantation, "Starlight, Moonlight. I hope to see a ghost tonight!"

Her goal was to catch a glimpse of the ghosts, but not to let them catch her. If she got too close to where the ghosts were hiding, they'd jump up and chase her. Then she'd have to race back to the steps before being touched by the ghosts, or suffer results that were too scary to think about.

Wags leapt out of Bea's lap and charged toward the garage with Bea trailing. When Wags spotted the "ghosts," she began barking and circling.

"Uh oh, come quick, Wags, before they catch us!" Bea called out. They turned and ran back toward the steps, but Brambles, spry for his age, and Auggie caught up with them first.

"Gotcha!" said Brambles, catching Bea in his arms and lifting her off her feet in a joyful hug. "Oh no!" Bea cried out in mock fear.

Wags was easy for the "ghost" Auggie to

catch. She wanted to be caught, by a Tiggy-wiggle of course, so she sprung into his arms and began to lick him wildly. "Guess you're not too scared of ghosts," he said.

"She's our bravest little girl," said Bea.

"Yes, she has a courageous heart, this one," said Brambles.

Inside the porch, Hortense was comforting her dear husband with her arms around his shoulders as he slumped back on the comfy, well-padded wicker chair.

"She's so little, you'll hardly notice her," she said in her soft, soothing voice. "I'll make sure the kids feed and walk her, and I'll be very strict (*Not*, she thought) about house privileges. She'll stay in the family room, off the furniture, and she won't get any food from the table. She'll be kenneled when we're gone. She won't cost us much. As you well know, we've got plenty of dog food."

Billy just moaned in near defeat, resting his head on his good wife's shoulder.

"*Temporary*, Hortense, my pet. It's just until we find her family."

There was little he wouldn't do for her, but he really loathed the idea of a dog in the house, even if it was only temporary.

. . .

With Francis and Vladi gone, the atmosphere at Fagin's Resort was tranquil. Cookie enjoyed nights like this alone with Ani. She loved her luxurious bedroom with a balcony overlooking the pool and golf course beyond it, the gauzy pink curtains undulated with the gentle, warm summer breezes. The residents of The Dogg House had settled down for the night, so Cookie enjoyed the peaceful quiet, cuddling with Ani on her emperor-sized bed with gold satin sheets and coverlet. She lay back on a mountain of pillows with her copy of *Town and Country* magazine, imagining the luxuries she would buy for herself for Francis's birthday in November. Maybe a cruise. Maybe another car. Possibly a restaurant. She tried to think of anything other than her husband's rage over that lost dog. She hoped he and Craig would find the pesky dog pronto.

. . .

While Endwell slept, Francis cruised the streets with Craig as his lookout for Wags. Here and there, a cat dashed by, a lone opossum waddled across the road, and night birds sang, but for the most part, the town was still. Even the squirrels were in for the night. Craig and his uncle didn't speak. There was nothing to say. The teenager lamented his damaged laptop and felt anxious to think of spending a night without a game to play. Nothing in the natural world attracted him. If it wasn't on a screen, he wasn't interested.

Francis drove slowly down every street and avenue in the small town and then several miles in every direction on the country highways that snaked through hilly farmlands. Fog settled in the dips of the roadways, making it difficult to see, but Francis didn't care. He expected his nephew to have X-ray vision. Eventually, as dawn was breaking, they gave up the search and returned to Fagin's Resort. Cranky Franky, true to his nickname, stomped into the house, leaving Craig to walk the three miles back to his parents' cat-filled home overlooking the freeway. The comforting hum of cars whizzing by outside his window might assuage his anxiety over seeing his uncle later in the day, and see him he certainly would. Craig knew that the old weasel wouldn't leave him alone until they recaptured #63. Maybe his parents would let him use their old Cadillac to widen the search. They liked to keep in good with their Cruikshank cousins, thinking that one day their solicitude would pay off like winning the lottery.

Walking down Lilac Lane past The Wishing Well, Craig became aware of an earthly fragrance on the wind that was surprisingly calming. For the first time in his life, he noticed the songs of crickets and night birds on the prairie. He'd never before been conscious of the natural world. It couldn't compare with the earsplitting music he was used to, but there was something rather pleasant about it.

. . .

After Brambles sauntered off to his own abode, the Tiggywiggles relaxed following all the excitement of Woofstock and finding their precious new dog. They went up to their bedrooms for well-earned sleep while Wags, penned in the family room, curled up on a fluffy pillow, blissful for the first time in her life. Before long, Bea and Auggie, laden with sleeping bags and pillows, joined her on the floor, encircling their treasured new friend. Upstairs, as Billy drifted off in his wife's cozy arms, his nightly snoring blared like a morning bugle call. Hortense smiled. Wags seemed to close the circle of her world, and she was immensely content.

Chapter 9

Wags at Home

Come morning, Hortense laughed softly, finding her children asleep on the family room floor with Wags, who got up when she appeared and greeted her enthusiastically. Hortense led Wags into the kitchen and opened the back door to let her scamper out for important dog business. Hortense wondered if she'd come back, but Wags was no fool; as soon as she was done, she raced back and danced around her new mom's feet. Hortense started making breakfast quietly so as not to wake her loved ones.

Billy slept in, snoring like the lead trumpeter for Tower of Power, a band with a powerful horn section. When the kids were up and dressed, they chattered happily over a breakfast of crepes with a dab of butter, a squeeze of lemon juice, and a sprinkle of powdered sugar, their mom's favorite. Hortense stood at the stove, flipping the crepes and stacking them on a plate covered with a towel to keep them warm. She nibbled on hers, fully enjoying a sunny start to the day.

"We'll have to get Wags a collar, a leash, and a kennel," she said. "You guys want to come to Au Naturel Pet Store with me this morning?"

"Sure! Can Wags come too?" Auggie said.

"She'll have to so we can fit her for her collar. You two will have to hold her in the car until we get her properly outfitted and buy a carrier to keep her safe in the car."

They finished breakfast, cleaned the dishes, and left a note by a plate of crepes for Billy. Then they piled into their aqua-blue Prius for Wags's first car ride. She was game, sticking her nose so far out the window that Hortense thought the wind might blow her right out of the car.

"Let's roll up the windows a bit. We don't want to lose her before we find her family."

"We don't want to lose her period," said Bea. Hortense agreed but said nothing.

Faith Carmichael greeted the happy family when they entered her business, the Au Naturel Pet Store.

"Wonders never cease. I never thought I'd see the Tiggywiggles with a dog!"

"It's just temporary, Faith," said Hortense. "She got lost during Woofstock, so we talked Billy into letting us keep her until we can find her family."

Faith laughed. "Well, I never!"

"How'd it go for you at Woofstock?"

"Fair to middling," Faith responded, not wanting to brag. Next to Christmas and National Dog Day, Woofstock was her biggest money maker. Her booth was always teeming with customers.

"Maybe you'll do better next year," said Hortense hopefully. "What do you have in a collar, leash, car carrier, and a couple of dog gates for Wags?"

"We sold out of a lot of things," Faith admitted. "She'll take an extra small. There's a black skull and crossbones collar and a sequined pink leash. Will that do? I still have some dog gates and a couple of crates."

Faith handed the collar to Hortense, who handed it to Bea. "See if it fits, honey bunch," she said.

Faith said, "It should be snug with room for two fingers."

Bea fitted the collar on Wags and attached the leash. Auggie giggled and said, "She looks silly."

"It's just temporary, remember," their mom said. To Faith, she said, "We'll take it all."

Wags pranced around the pet shop, admiring herself in the reflection of the storefront window. As she was turning back towards her new family, two mournful eyes appeared in the window. Nomad! How could she have forgotten him? Without his help, she'd never have become a Tiggywiggle! She pounced on the window, barking madly at her friend on the other side.

"I'll send Billy over with the Range Rover to pick up the dog gates and restock your supply of dog food, Faith," Hortense said. Then she noticed Wags bouncing off the window and circling anxiously. "What's with Wags?" she asked the kids.

"She sees another dog outside and is going nuts," said Bea.

"I can see that," her mom commented.

"That's the stray who hangs around here begging for food," said Faith. "I call him Nomad."

Nomad and Wags had their paws up on the window, separated only by the glass. Both were wagging their tails vigorously.

As a customer entered, Wags pulled away from the children and dashed out the door, dragging her new leash behind her. She nearly knocked Nomad over with her buoyant energy. They nuzzled each other like the not-so-long lost friends they were.

"I suppose you're a Tiggywiggle now," Nomad said wistfully.

"Yes, it's wonderful! But Billy, the dad, says it's only until they find my family."

"Old Cruikshank and his nephew Craig were out all night looking for you."

"What if he puts up 'Lost Dog' posters?"

"You don't have to worry about that. Cranky Franky doesn't want anyone to know he's running a puppy mill."

"What about you?"

"What about me? I'm alone again, naturally."

The Tiggywiggles had come out of the store to see what the fuss was about. Wags looked at them as if she were begging for a cookie and then circled around Nomad, wagging her tail enthusiastically.

"Oh no you don't, Wags," Hortense said sternly. "We're already over our limit with you!"

"We can't just leave him here, Momzella," Bea pleaded.

"He's all matted up like Wags was. We gotta help him!" Auggie said.

"No. The answer is no. Your father wouldn't have it."

"He doesn't have to know . . ." said Bea conspiratorially.

Faith had come out of the store to see what all the ruckus was about.

"Faith, we'll need a harness and leash for him, and a lawyer for me!" Hortense said, defeated. "Billy will divorce me for sure if he finds out!" The crate was barely large enough for the two dogs, way too many dogs for Billy Tiggywiggle.

. . .

Hortense called Billy, asking him to pick up the gates and restock Faith's supply of Frenchy's Dog Food to give them a chance to get back to the house without being seen. Auggie and Bea were delighted with their two new dogs, chatting with them in the car on the way home. Hortense's stomach tensed, knowing that she was violating her husband's one demand. She knew that it was wrong, but that it was right at the same time.

. . .

Without a laptop and a game to play, Craig was more lethargic than usual. He didn't want to get out of bed, but Uncle Francis had woken him out of a nightmare about a bleak world without electronics. He was on the phone, demanding that Craig continue the search, making it clear that he would stuff Craig into #63's cage in The Dogg House if he didn't find her soon.

Craig dragged himself out of his house and aimlessly continued the hunt on foot for the darn dog that had caused all the trouble. His parents needed their car for the Midwest Cataholics Convention. Uncle Francis had given him a photo of #63 that had been taken to show off her fine features to prospective sires. Craig was supposed to show it around the neighborhood to help find her.

Francis was afraid someone might catch on that he had a puppy mill if he himself went out in daylight in search of the dog who'd be making him buckets of money in the future. He puffed impatiently on Cuban cigars in his office, waiting for Craig to return with his dog. *That knucklehead better find her*, he thought ruefully. He wondered if he should've hired a professional dog handler, but Craig was cheap, and so was Francis.

Craig was on his hands and knees looking under a fence on Lilac Lane just a few houses away from The Wishing Well when Hortense and the kids drove by.

Auggie called out, "Hey, Craig, look what we've got!" Craig wasn't interested in anything those foolish Tiggywiggles had, so he ignored Auggie, not even raising his head to acknowledge the boy.

"Shhh," Hortense warned urgently. "He's the Cruikshanks' nephew, and they better not know we have either dog! Got it?"

"Yeah, Momzella," said Auggie, who wanted to share his news with the world.

"What about Uncle Brambles?" Bea wanted to know.

"He's the only one we *can* trust," said her mom, ruminating for a moment. "That's it! We'll get Bram to take Nomad until we can straighten this whole dog situation out. Thank heavens for Uncle Brambles. I really don't know what we'd do without him."

"He could say that Nomad is the model for one of his sculptures," Auggie offered.

"True that, honey bunch, but the less said, the better all around. Let's go see Bram."

. . .

Rooting around in what he thought were weeds, Craig caught sight of a couple of monarch butterflies floating on the air like paper airplanes. He caught himself smiling at their beauty for a moment and then remembered the task that would get him back his longed-for laptop. He looked up, hoping to see that small, furry being, but a heavenly butterfly winged past him instead.

. . .

Uncle Brambles was working on the rear end of a red clay sculpture of a Bassett Hound when the Tiggywiggle entourage arrived. The statue was on a large lazy Susan that Brambles could move easily to do his work. His hands, arms, and once-white overalls were dappled with red clay. He was so absorbed in getting the tail end of the dog just right, he welcomed them in without looking up.

"Welcome, welcome, treasured associates! Come in and see my latest work of DArt!" Brambles said, making a whoosh with his hands over the Bassett Hound's rear quarters and turning the lazy Susan toward his visitors so they could admire his work.

"What!" he gasped, turning toward them. "What have we here? Two dogs? What's next, a team of sled dogs?"

"No, Uncle Bram," said Hortense. "Just one more. He's Wags's friend. He was hanging around outside the pet store, and Wags wouldn't let us leave without him."

"I know this fellow," said Brambles, reaching over to pet Nomad. "He comes by for a drink of water at my trough, and I've given him bits of my sandwich now and then, but I didn't dare bring him in. Billy's rules, you know."

"Yes, I know all too well, Uncle, but you'll have to take him for the time being. Wags won't settle down if her pal is left out in the cold."

"My pleasure indeed. I hate to go behind our dear Billy's back, but as you say, it's only temporary. This poor fellow does look a little seedy. Oh well," he said, giving in. "We can't turn him away." Brambles was secretly thrilled to have any dog for any length of time. He said to Nomad, "So what will we do with you now?"

"I know," Bea piped up. "Give the dog a bath!"

"Indeed," said Brambles. "That's the ticket. If Billy finds out I'm harboring a dog on his property, I'll just say that he's a model for one of my sculptures."

"That was my idea," Auggie piped up.

"A fine idea indeed," said Brambles. "But . . ." he and Hortense said in unison, "the less said, the better."

. . .

Loading cases of dog food into their beat-up Range Rover, Billy thought of stopping by Uncle Brambles's, as he often did in times of trouble to talk things through. This was indeed one of those times. He was beyond irritated to have a dog in the house, but the joy of his wife and children was hard to ignore. He was glad to have an errand to take his mind off the whole mess. As he headed over to the Au Naturel Pet Store, he noticed that odd nephew of the Cruikshanks' poking around in some bushes down the lane. *What is his name?* Billy puzzled. *Greg? Clyde?* The kid was obviously searching for something. *Maybe his brain*, Billy thought, chuckling to himself. Anyone who had anything to do with the Cruikshanks surely had to be empty-headed.

. . .

Now that Nomad was safely ensconced with Uncle Brambles, Hortense, the kids, and Wags returned to The Wishing Well. It was another lovely day, so they had a picnic on the lawn. Dadoid had made pan bagnat, a long French baguette stuffed with a delicious salade niçoise of greens, olives, and tuna before leaving for the pet store. His note said to go ahead and eat. He'd have his lunch later. The humans feasted on that while Wags enjoyed a bowl of Frenchy's Surf 'n' Turf that she speedily wolfed down.

"What do you know, Wags?" Auggie inquired. "Do you know how to sit, walk on a leash, lie down?"

"Let's see," said Hortense. "Wags, sit!" she said brightly.

Wags jumped up and turned around in circles.

"I know," said Bea. "She needs some incentive." Bea fished some tuna out of her sandwich and showed it to Wags. "Wags, sit!"

Wags flopped down on all fours, rolled onto her back, and wiggled her paws in the air in the grass.

"Guess she hasn't had much training," said Auggie mirthfully. "But I don't care. She's my new *beast* friend forever!"

. . .

At Fagin's Resort, Cookie began to stew. Her husband and Vladi were in his office, grumbling over the lost dog. Cookie was used to his grumbling about the outrageous stories on the Fix Network that was now blaring from the office. Normally, she and her husband groused about the injustices in the world together. Now, the problem was on her turf, and she felt left out of the action. Craig couldn't find his own nose in a mirror, so it was unlikely that he'd find #63. She needed to do something herself.

"Francis!" she called to her husband. She couldn't tell over the din if he'd heard, so she wrote him a note saying she and Ani were joining the search. The twosome settled into her white luxury sedan and headed downtown. Maybe that pet store lady . . . what was her name? Patience? Maybe she would know something.

Billy Tiggywiggle was just leaving Au Naturel when Cookie and Ani swept by.

"Oh, hello, Cookie," he said. "I'm just on my way back to work."

"Well then, off you go," Cookie responded briskly.

Billy left with dispatch. He was looking forward to burying himself in work to avoid the whole dog dilemma. There was plenty to do: sorting and storing festival supplies and receipts for Hortense, making the donations to the various charities, and all sorts of busy-work perfectly suited to distract him.

"Bye, Cookie," he said, but she had already turned her attention to Faith, so he forged on his way, closing the door behind him.

"Patience, have you seen this little Yorkie?" Cookie asked, pulling the photo of Wags out of her expensive Kate Spade hobo bag.

"Didn't know you had a Yorkie, Mrs. Cruikshank," said Faith, choosing not to correct Cookie on her name.

"We don't. I'm asking for a friend."

"Uh-huh. Fine-looking dog," Faith observed.

"Yes, yes, so have you seen her?" Cookie asked impatiently of the woman she thought was named Patience.

"Oh, I've seen many Yorkies in my time."

"What about this one?"

"This one could be a poster pup for Yorkies."

"So, you've seen her?"

"Maybe. I see a lot of dogs, ya know."

"Well, if you do see her, call me. She's scheduled to be bred with Champion Sir Lancelot Lickalot this Saturday, so we haven't got a lot of time. Here's my card."

"Oh, I've got your number, Mrs. Cruikshank. It's on TV all the time. 'Amazin' Fagin's. Call 800-800-0800.'"

"I'll leave you some cards anyway . . . good to know that the advertising pays off."

"Indeedy do, Mrs. Cruikshank." Faith, like George Washington, couldn't tell a lie, but that didn't mean she had to spill the beans. She smirked to herself, picturing the rapturous Tiggywiggle kids playing with the dog belonging to the Cruikshanks' "friend." Like they had any friends! So, who *could* that little Yorkie belong to? She seemed to be right at home with the Tiggywiggles.

Chapter 10

Wags Asleep on the Job

Endwell was a village of 12,372 inhabitants settled along Sioux Creek, which meandered through it, eventually spilling into Lake Michigan to the east. It was so small, it would be hard to hide anything there, even the smallest of dogs.

. . .

By Tuesday afternoon, everyone was at rest at The Wishing Well. Hortense drifted off, resting on the davenport in the family room with Wags on her shoulder. The dog gate was in place at the door as per her agreement with Billy. Tired out from all the excitement of Woofstock and a dog in their lives, Bea and Auggie dozed on wicker couches on the porch. The peaceful, happy energy of the house overtook Billy. He too lay down for a snooze in the living room.

Wags snuggled on Hortense's shoulder, but wasn't ready for a nap. It seemed like she'd napped her whole life away until coming here. She got up, descended on a cascade of pillows to the floor, and began exploring. Out of their own money, Bea and Auggie had bought her some toys that lay strewn about on the floor. It seemed that they wanted her to do something with them, but not having had toys before, she didn't know what. She sniffed them in passing—they were a puzzlement. A refreshing bowl of water awaited her in the corner. She drank from it gratefully.

There wasn't much at her level to explore. Other than the pillows on the davenport and the toys, there was little of interest. Hortense, being something of a neat freak, kept even the family room fresh and clean with everything in its place. Even the counter stools at the tiki bar were neatly tucked away. Separating Wags from the rest of the house was the sturdy dog gate. Given her negative experience at The Dogg House, she was not a fan of cages, fences, or barriers of any kind. She sat for several minutes, observing the gate. She didn't care about what was on the other side; she just didn't like being prevented from it.

Wags tested the gate with both front paws. Solid. It didn't budge. Then she tried gnawing on the vinyl-coated fencing, but that got her nowhere. The gate was five times her height, but she thought of nothing but freedom as she grabbed onto the mesh using her teeth and claws like mountain climbers' crampons. She was fearless as she reached up for higher and higher rungs until she was teetering on the top of the fence and gravity pushed her over to the other side. The fall was jarring, but not painful.

She hit the ground and rolled over and over until she finally came to a stop in a long hallway. Wags trotted to the doorway of a majestic room festooned with colorful paintings and a large collection of family pictures on a baby grand piano. The walls were a pale, tranquil periwinkle blue. Late-afternoon sunlight bathed the furniture in a warm golden glow.

There was a long couch with its back to her, and she was about to saunter off to explore the rest of the house when a loud snort caught her attention. It was Billy, sounding like the bugle horn of a military call to arms, followed by deep rumblings. Asleep, he could've provided the trumpet passages in a rousing John Philip Sousa march with his snores. Fortunately, Hortense was used to her husband's "night music." At night, she wove his brassy sounds into dreams of her family's band at a fine concert hall full of fans.

Wags, unfamiliar with most human proclivities, padded curiously toward Billy on a thick rug that looked like a watercolor painting. Uh-oh. It was the man she had landed on at the agility trials at Woofstock! The one who hated dogs and wouldn't allow them in his home! Yikes! She jumped back in shock and then nervously ran around and around the couch until she could settle down to assess the situation. The human did not respond to her movements, continuing to snore boisterously.

Wags's nose twitched as she sat quietly observing her human nemesis. They did have a sort of bond of opposites; he hated dogs, and she was not so sure she liked humans, with the exception of the other Tiggywiggles and Uncle Brambles, of course. Wags and Billy were two peas in an uncomfortable pod. The peacefulness of the atmosphere around her began to have a soporific effect on her. She hopped onto one of the pillows Billy had knocked off the couch. She scratched it and circled around it, making her bed comfortable. She was about to drift off when she felt the warmth of the recumbent human.

Life had been either too hot or too cold at The Dogg House. Although the Tiggywiggle home was at a comfortable temperature, she gravitated toward Billy's aura of comfort. Using the pillows as her staircase, she tentatively wiggled her way up to the couch right beneath

Billy's chin. So far, so good. Like she had with the pillows, she circled three times before plopping down underneath Billy's chin. She expelled a sigh of relief after a journey well-traveled and went to sleep breathing in tempo with Billy's rhythmic brass concerto.

. . .

Hortense had an inner clock that alerted her to her many duties, like waking the children and preparing the family meals. She rose to a sitting position, yawned deeply, and stretched her arms overhead. The kids were still sleeping, and she had no intention of waking them until she was ready to serve their dinner. They needed their sleep. In her dreams, a small Yorkie had sailed in the air like a busy bee around The Wishing Well, landing on Billy's head. His shock in the dream was what woke her. Still cloaked in drowsiness, she noted that something was missing, but she didn't know what.

She gazed all around. Observing her children in the family room brought a smile to her lovely face. Then she noticed the dog gate. That was it! The dog was not a dream, but where *was* she? Hortense got up and explored every nook and cranny of the area to no avail. No dog. *How could Wags have disappeared?* she wondered since the dog gate was still in place. Maybe Wags was hiding. Or maybe this really was a dream. As she pondered this conundrum, she said softly aloud, "Where, oh where, could my little dog be?" *My little dog.* She smiled at the thought of owning the little dog who had so quickly won her heart. She too hoped they'd never find the owners.

. . .

As Wags nestled into Billy's neck, right under his chin, he sighed a happy exhalation of comfort. His dreams of The Wishing Well being stormed by armies of canines faded, and peace shone over his homestead in his mind. Wags snored softly, and Billy's snores softened to barely perceptible exhalations. The two seemed to unconsciously bond in melodic harmony. The silence startled Hortense, who was as used to Billy's snoring as she was to her coffee in the morning. *Oh no!* she thought, wondering if the intrusion of a dog in their home had resulted in a heart attack. She rushed to check on Billy in his favorite oasis in the living room.

To her amazement, instead of a dead husband on the davenport, she found a blissful pair, man and dog, happily melded together. Wags awoke at Hortense's arrival and began to wag her tail into Billy's nose, then leapt from her resting place and jumped on Hortense, begging her to pick her up, which she did automatically. At the same time, Billy awoke with a start and shook his head to unscramble his brain. Were the kids playing some kind of game to wake him up? What was that hairy thing that thumped on his face? As he lifted his bleary eyes to consider his beautiful wife, he noticed the culprit. Wags! The dog! What in heaven's name was she doing in the living room? "What?" he exclaimed.

"Honestly, honeybun," Hortense assured him, "we had her holed up in the family room behind a dog gate. I don't know how she could've gotten out. It must be a gravitational pull to you, you handsome dog. When I found you, the two of you were entwined in blissful slumber. And you weren't snoring like a freight train going through a tunnel! Your silence scared me. I thought maybe you'd had a heart attack! I'll put her right back in the family room."

Carrying sleep with them like cozy blankets, the kids awoke and walked sleepily into the living room. The scene before them startled them into alert consciousness. "Oh no, Dadoid!" cried Auggie. "We had her locked up," Bea said urgently, completing her brother's sentence.

"Well, this just won't do," said Billy, now fully awake. "It just won't do. I ask just one thing of you, to keep dogs out of our home, and here she is right in the living room ..."

"Snuggling with you on the davenport," said Hortense, finishing her husband's sen-

127

tence. "And for the first time since we've been married, you were sleeping like a baby, barely snoring at all."

"It just won't do," said Billy stubbornly. "Kids, go out and take her for a walk before dinner. Maybe you'll find her owners and we can get back to normal."

"But Dadoid!" Bea implored. "Having a dog *is* normal."

"Not for the Tiggywiggles," Billy said with irritation fading as he observed his wife and children juggling that wiggly ball of fur. "Go," he said somewhat firmly before he lost his resolve.

"OK, Dadoid, we're going," said Auggie.

"I'll get her leash," said Bea dispiritedly.

"No pouting, children. Your dad is breaking his one major rule of the house. Let's enjoy our time with Wags but get her back home to her family as soon as we can," said Hortense, the diplomat of the family.

"But, Momzella, she *is* home," said Auggie.

"*Temporary* home. Now, go!" their mother directed, stopping to fondle Wags's ears, who was in Auggie's arms smiling like she'd won the lottery. In her world, she had.

. . .

The children walked Wags over to Uncle Brambles's cottage to pick up Nomad. He and Wags were happy to see each other, tails wagging, tumbling one over the other, and smiling with their tongues hanging out. Nomad had never felt better. Brambles had given him a bath with warm water and gentle soap that didn't sting his eyes and then spent hours gently working out all the debris of his coat. Next was a glorious walk in the woods, dinner, and a rawhide chewy for dessert. Nomad was a new dog.

"Off to find Wags's family?" Brambles asked the kids.

"Yeah, yeah," they responded dismally.

"Well, I, for one, hope you never find them!" Brambles said, conspiring with them.

This thought perked them up. They hooked Nomad up to his new leash and took off with both dogs down Lilac Lane. When they saw people or a car coming, they ducked behind bushes, pulling the dogs in with them so as not to be seen. They did a quick turn around Endwell's downtown without being discovered by people too busy to worry about the whereabouts of an errant dog. Heading west toward Fagin's Resort, they heard Francis Cruikshank's growling lowrider coming up the rise. They crashed into thorny shrubbery just in time. Scratched and bleeding a bit, they sat on their haunches, Bea holding Wags and Auggie hugging Nomad.

"There's Craig Cruikshank in the car with that stinky, old Cranky Franky," Bea whispered to her brother.

"Like uncle, like nephew, they're both bad news," Auggie whispered back. The foursome stayed in their uncomfortable hiding place until Cruikshank and Craig were out of sight down the lengthy driveway and onto the road driving toward town. The children and the dogs escaped detection by taking a path into the woods between Fagan's Resort and The Wishing Well. They all felt relieved and took in deep breaths of the pungent, pine-scented air. Since, technically, they had done their due diligence of looking for Wags's family, they headed back toward Uncle Brambles's cottage, taking their time, dogs and children examining their environment with joy and curiosity. Nomad found a stick longer than he was and trotted proudly with it barely fitting in his jaws. Wags found something wonderfully stinky to roll in and wiggled her back into it with furious enthusiasm.

"Oh, Wags!" Bea admonished. "You're going to need another bath!" Of course, Wags didn't care. She paraded through the thicket with her head held high and a look of smugly grand satisfaction.

"Hey, Bea, look, there's a couple puffballs next to that dead tree trunk!" Auggie, the discoverer, said. Bea took both leashes, and Auggie collected as many of the large white mushrooms as he could fit in his T-shirt pulled up from the bottom into a makeshift bag.

"Dadoid will love those!" said Bea.

"There's enough for Uncle Brambles too,"

said Auggie, leading the way back to their uncle's cottage.

They found Brambles, intent on carving his latest statue out of a wooden tree stump. It looked a lot like Nomad. Although their uncle had a naturally cheerful nature, the infusion of a real dog whom he could pet and play with heightened his happiness immeasurably. Nomad pulled the leash right out of Bea's hand and bolted to Brambles, nearly toppling him over. Brambles stumbled back to his workbench to steady himself while Nomad attacked him with kisses. Wags pulled at her leash to join in the fun. Both of the kids laughed at the happy scene.

"Uncle Brambles, look what we found!" said Auggie proudly, pulling his shirt outward to show the bounty he'd collected from the woods.

"Oh, that's quite a treasure trove. Your dad will be ecstatic," said Brambles.

"There's plenty for you and for us," said Auggie. "I'll go in and put some on your kitchen table."

"Capital, dear boy, capital. Nomad and I will have a feast. I have a stew on for supper, and mushrooms are just what was missing."

As Auggie ran into the house, Brambles addressed Bea with seriousness. "Where are you at finding Wags's people?"

"We walked her all over town, and nobody claimed her."

"Good. But I'm surprised no one came forward with any information. Ours is a small town, and few things go missing from someone's eyes. Are you sure you walked the whole village?"

"Well . . ."

"Well?"

"Well, we did, but we ducked into the bushes anytime we saw someone coming," said Bea sheepishly, as she was normally an obedient child. Brambles snorted a laugh involuntarily.

Auggie had heard the conversation and had rejoined them with downcast eyes, expecting their uncle's reproach.

"Well done!" said Brambles.

"You aren't mad?"

"You aren't going to tell Momzella and Dadoid?"

"Heavens, no. It's just what I'd have done meself!" he said conspiratorially, talking like a pirate.

"Oh, Uncle, we don't want to lose her," said Bea.

"She's so happy with us. She's family already," said Auggie.

"Seems to me someone ought to have been out looking for her and posting 'Lost Dog' flyers. Fine dog like her."

"Yeah! One for all and all for one!" said Auggie and fist-bumped with the others.

. . .

Back at The Wishing Well, Hortense was comforting her husband.

"I'm making you Beach Burgers for dinner," she said buoyantly.

"You're trying to win me over, and it won't do. Do you have the avocado?"

"Yes, of course. It's perfectly ripened the way you like it. *And*, I have fresh honeybunions from the farm *and* Mrs. Bump's rolls. It'll all be fine. The kids are out looking for Wags's owners. Such a fine little dog, you'd think someone would be out looking for her and putting up posters."

"I'll put up posters if we don't find the owners soon."

"The kids will be home soon. Let's just have dinner and turn in for the night. Enough excitement for one day." Thinking of the slumber she looked forward to, she thought about Billy's snoring. That and his hatred of dogs were the only stumbling blocks in their solid, loving relationship. Although she loved to snuggle in her husband's arms, sometimes the alarming volume of his snoring kept her awake so long that she'd sneak out of bed and catch a couple hours of sleep on the couch in the family room. It was at its worst when Billy was stressed. Tonight, it would be as loud as a Metallica concert. They'd tried many remedies, but nothing worked. Wags had done something to soothe Billy into quiet slumber. If she could do it once, maybe she could do it again, Hortense thought.

"Here come the kids. We'll put Wags in the family room, and then we can have dinner. It looks like Auggie found some puffballs. I'll sauté them in butter the way you like them."

"Thanks, my love," said Billy listlessly.

The family had dinner in the kitchen while Wags savored an exquisite bowl of Frenchy's Dog Food in the family room. Surf 'n' Turf again. Better than dinner at Red Lobster.

. . .

"Oh where, oh where, could that little monster dog be?" Cookie hissed softly under her breath. That dog was more trouble that she was worth. "Let her go," Cookie said to her husband after he'd returned from the hunt with Craig grumpier than normal, if that was possible. He'd gone out during the day against his own best judgment just to find the little beast.

"We've got plenty of other dogs, and car sales are going great. What's the fuss over that one little ball of fuzz? Craig's gone home, and it's getting dark. Give it up, at least for today, and let's go to the country club for dinner. Your favorite steak tartar at the Kennelworth Club will fortify you."

"Errr," he growled.

"I don't know why you won't let me put up some posters. We have a license to breed and sell dogs. We might push the limits of the law, but let them try to prosecute! We can say we're hobby breeders with a lot of hobbies," Cookie said, giggling at her own deviousness. "Come on, let's go."

. . .

At The Wishing Well, the Tiggywiggles were all in their pjs and ready for bed. The kids insisted on sleeping in the family room with Wags while their parents went upstairs to their bedroom. The nanosecond Billy's head hit the pillow, his snoring erupted into a jarring trumpet-like solo. Hortense tried to sleep. She was bone-tired from Woofstock and all the shenanigans since then. She hoped to drift off into delicious recumbent dreamland, but every time she thought she was floating into sleep, Billy let out a fearsome noise. There would be no sleep for her this night. Unless . . .

Quietly, Hortense disengaged herself from Billy's gentle arms and quietly padded downstairs on tiptoes. From the ambient light of a full moon shining through the window, she could see that the kids were sound asleep on the floor in the family room. Wags, who'd been sleeping on top of Bea's head, bounded toward the gate, wagging her tail furiously.

"Come here, little one, and work your magic on Billy again," she said, picking up Wags, enjoying the dainty dog's silky fur and cold nose bumping into her neck.

As quietly as she had come downstairs, Hortense mounted the staircase and re-entered their bedroom undetected by her husband, who sounded like he was practicing for a band concert at the White House. Hortense put Wags down on the bed on her side and gently pushed her toward Billy's neck. Wags immediately took to this new sleeping arrangement, curling in a ball under the chin of the man who hated her. Hortense sat on the bed for a few moments and was astounded by the silence. It worked again! Wags was the cure for Billy's snoring! Hortense set her internal clock to wake before Billy so she could return Wags to the family room before Billy awoke. She lay down, the weight of the world lifted, and she slept more deeply than she had since she married her treasured husband, not knowing about his snoring.

. . .

It was a peaceful night in Endwell. A chorus of crickets rose in volume as fog settled into the deep kettles of the land and the moonlight etched the crests of the hilly moraines against a clear, starry sky. The Sioux Creek whispered to the cosmos as it gently wended its way toward Lake Michigan. The heat of the day lifted, leaving a refreshing chill to the air. No one was snoring in Endwell that evening.

Chapter 11

Collared

Mourning doves cooed the coming dawn as little wood thrushes issued their quiet, flute-like reveille. The sun peeked over the eastern horizon and woke up bright-blue morning glories that burst out on a trellis on the south side of The Wishing Well. Squirrels and chipmunks dashed hither and thither in their quest for breakfast. The humans at The Wishing Well were slow to rise from their profound slumbers. As planned, Hortense arose first, stealthily lifted sleepy Wags from her resting place next to Billy, and took her downstairs and out to the yard for a morning jaunt. It all seemed so natural to Hortense.

She couldn't imagine life without Wags anymore.

. . .

At Fagin's Resort, the atmosphere was so dark and brooding, it seemed to draw storm clouds over the grounds. Cookie awoke first, looking forward to her work that day: filming a commercial for the car dealership. Ani and Vladi joined her in the kitchen. When she let them out into the yard, they paid no attention to the distant cacophony of The Dogg House.

Wrested from bad dreams about escaped dogs by the aroma of Cookie's morning brew, Cranky Franky sluggishly met the day with his usual petulance. He ruefully considered another day in search of that little gremlin, thanks to his idiot nephew who let her go. The mating on Saturday was just three days away, and the dog would need to be groomed before then. He rumbled aloud like a wild animal scouting its prey. Craig, the oaf, was still sleeping when Francis called to demand that he report immediately to Fagin's Resort for another day of dog hunting.

Craig had suffered bad dreams of his uncle Francis smashing all his electronics with the guitar that he never played. A happy little dog floated through the dreams, ever out of reach, until the phone rang and his mother shouted loud enough to wake the lazy teenager. He couldn't escape his uncle asleep or awake, and he knew he wouldn't be able to replace his computer until they found the little dog that haunted him like an evil wraith.

It was the dog's fault that his game was so brutally interrupted and his laptop was destroyed. Craig, who'd been hoping to get a virtual reality machine, didn't even have the equipment to get back to his old game now. He'd have to replace the laptop and start all over again, working his way up the levels with ever-increasing challenges. How rude of his uncle! How rude of the mutt! Somehow, he had to find her. He slogged out of bed, slipping into his rumpled clothing on the floor. He didn't bother to brush his teeth, comb his hair, or stop for breakfast. He was on a mission that had snatched him from the cyberworld and thrust him unwillingly into the real world he so diligently sought to avoid.

The maddening dog seemed to have disappeared into thin air. *Where could she have gone to?* Craig wondered, again frustrated by the mere thought of her. The search was so exasperating! As he trudged through a park along Sioux Creek en route to Fagin's Resort, elegant monarch butterflies and tiny white moths flitted everywhere over the mouths of late-summer flowers. The automatons he was used to in his virtual world made bold, jerky movements. The butterflies sailed along the gentle breezes so gracefully, he thought they were sort of cool, although he longed to escape back into his computer games.

. . .

The Tiggywiggles enjoyed their breakfast with special zest. Better rested than he could ever remember, Billy was in the pink. He looked forward to his day of work and play. Hortense, the company accountant, needed to reconcile the many receipts Billy had accumulated from Woofstock. She loved the logic and order of her work. For her, it was a relaxing enterprise. She was naturally cheerful, but her husband's sense of well-being added an extra measure of joy. Auggie and Bea played happily with Wags in the family room, looking forward to their morning jaunt, feeling more confident that they *wouldn't* find Wags's family.

"Dadoid, you look terrific," said Bea.

"I feel great, honey bunches of groats!" Billy was beaming, although he didn't know why he felt so good.

"You must be doing something right, dear heart," said Hortense to her husband, who was blissfully flipping pancakes and piling them on plates. "Your pancakes are especially good too!"

"It's the recipe from our camping trip guide in the Smokies. Cornmeal with fresh corn and buttermilk."

"I'll take mine with maple syrup," said Auggie.

"I'll have the green chili salsa and sour cream," said Bea.

"I'll have two of each," said Billy, and they all laughed.

After eating, the children were assigned clean-up duties since their dad had cooked. The twosome made quick work of washing and drying the dishes. As a Girl Scout, Bea was tasked with leaving a place better than she found it, so she ran outside and collected wildflowers for the table while Auggie put the dishes away. Then, they each dug into the stash of money they'd earned working at Woofstock, stuffing some of it into their pockets.

Feeling flush in every way, they liberated Wags from the family room, leashed her up, and skipped out the door toward downtown. Once again, they used alleys and backstreets to avoid detection. Eventually, they came out on Main Street just half a block away from Au Naturel Pet Store, where they were headed to buy more treats for Wags and Nomad. Pausing to admire all the wonderful things they could buy for Wags in the window, they didn't notice an ominous shadow coming up behind them.

"Hey," said Craig Cruikshank impatiently. "That's our dog!"

Flustered, Auggie played innocent. "What dog?"

"The dog you're holding!" Craig shouted at Bea.

"This dog?" Bea inquired, shivering with fear.

"Yeah, I'll take 'er," said Craig, grabbing for the leash. As he bent over and leaned forward, Wags jumped back. Craig lost his balance and fell on his face. "Why, I could smash that dog like a bug. What a nuisance!"

"But, Craig, you don't have any dogs. Everybody knows your mom is a cat collector."

"It's my uncle's dog."

"Your uncle Franky?" Auggie whispered, the words catching in his throat.

"That's Mr. Cruikshank to you, buddy," Craig snarled.

"No way," said Bea firmly, recovering her courage.

"Way. Gimme that leash," said Craig, this time leaning back on his heels and using his height to threaten the children. Wags shrieked and nipped him hard on the ankle like Nomad had done to make their escape.

Wags flew past the teen like a low jet. Bea and Auggie followed her, running past Craig. Since they didn't know what else to do, they all ran home. Their parents would know what to do. Craig, again schnockered by that little mutt, started to go after them but knew he couldn't catch up. *That's OK,* he sneered to himself. He'd go get Uncle Cranky Franky, and they'd show those Tiggywiggles a thing or two.

. . .

Billy was rummaging through the detritus from Woofstock in the garage when Wags and the kids whizzed by and ran into the kitchen, where their mom had her office.

Alarmed, Billy followed them inside. "What's going on?" said Hortense, surprised by the flurry of activity.

"Momzella, Momzella," the kids cried out in unison.

"Craig Cruikshank says that Wags is his uncle's dog!" Auggie said urgently as Bea broke down into sobs that shook her whole body. Wags wiggled at her feet, leaned in toward her, and kissed her shins.

"Francis Cruikshank, our neighbor?" Hortense asked. The kids nodded sorrowfully.

"Cranky Franky?" she asked again and got the same response.

"They have those Russian dogs," said Billy.

"Borzois," said Hortense, finishing his sentence as they often did with each other, being so in tune with each other's thoughts. "I didn't know they had any other dogs. Especially not one as small as Wags. Maybe Craig's been playing too many video games and is off his nut."

"But if this is Francis and Cookie's dog, we'll have to give her back," Billy said.

"Noooo," the kids whined together, both crying. Now Hortense had joined them.

"She fits in here. She likes it here. She hasn't tried to run away ... Oh, Billy, you can't let them take her away," Hortense implored Billy. "We love her and can't live without her."

"I told you it was temporary. Just until we found her family, and it seems we have."

. . .

The impressive growl of Francis's lowrider preceded him on the driveway to The Wishing Well. He pulled to a stop by the back door, and Craig got out and banged on the door. Wags barked, whined, and turned in panicked circles. It was that kid from The Dogg House. This could not be good news. Billy opened the door to Craig, who was flushed with anger.

"Uncle Cranky, er, Cruikshank says I got to take the dog back since I was the one who lost her," said Craig.

"Are you sure this is his dog, Craig?" Hortense tearfully asked.

"My uncle said to come and get her."

"But he's never had a little dog . . ."

"He does now," said Craig, pushing forward and grabbing Wags firmly by the collar. She twisted in his hands and snarled, baring her teeth and nipping his fingers with zest.

"Do you have any proof of ownership?" Billy asked. "We wouldn't want to return her to the wrong family."

"My uncle says she's chipped," said Craig over his shoulder, hustling out of the house to the car and jumping in with Wags struggling, scratching, and yelping. Francis gazed sideways at Hortense. She had spurned him once. *This is what she gets*, he thought with sneering delight. He rumbled along with the engine of his ride and started to drive away, confident of his rights in the matter.

. . .

Hortense and her children dripped unhappiness as they sat huddled together on the davenport, fingering Wags's meager belongings. How could these few heavenly days have disintegrated into this funeral scene?

"But you knew it was only temporary," Billy appealed to his family, which only made matters worse. Auggie chortled, "Arrrgh!"

"For heaven's sake, it's only a dog, not a member of the family," Billy said, digging the ditch he'd fallen into deeper.

Bea wailed, plopping her head on her mother's lap.

"Hortense, please, darling, be reasonable."

With a dark tone he'd never heard before in his wife, she hissed, "We *are* being reasonable. There is no reason why that ogre should have *our* dog!"

"But that's just my point. She *isn't* our dog." The threesome on the couch collapsed together in a heap of misery.

"You just don't know," said Hortense without looking up. "You just don't know the gifts that little dog has brought us." To her, their unconditional love made them Wags's rightful family.

The next half hour was as grief-stricken

as the wake for Hortense's beloved grandfather. When the tears dried up, the threesome drooped together, completely drained, with vacant looks on their faces.

"How about some custard?" Billy said brightly when he could no longer tolerate the silent grief of his loved ones. "I'll make banana splits. You love them!"

The threesome, heaving a mutual sigh, could not, in that moment, imagine having an appetite for anything.

"Well, I'll be a monkey's uncle!" said Billy, plopping down in his favorite chair.

"You don't know what we've lost," Hortense throatily whispered.

. . .

The atmosphere at Fagin's Resort was triumphant. Craig beamed at his own prowess in recapturing the errant dog. He thought about an upgrade to his system that he could now afford with the money he'd get from his uncle. Maybe even the virtual reality system of his dreams.

"Blessed be!" said Cookie as the entourage in the lowrider returned. "All's well that ends well for us in Endwell! Craig, go put that dog back in her cage! Francis, honey, come look at the vacation package to Pulao in *Town and Country*. You need a rest, dear."

He nodded grimly. This should never have happened in the first place. Craig would not get a penny for all the trouble he caused. As far as a scuba diving vacation in Pulao, he'd rather spend a week in The Dogg House than fly halfway around the planet to vacation in a humid, tropical nightmare full of snakes and mosquitos.

Craig returned Wags, struggling, biting, and yelping, to cage #63. He closed the door and locked it with a padlock, testing it to make sure she couldn't escape again. Then he rejoined Francis and Cookie in their spacious three-season room. Craig looked at his uncle expectantly but got only a scowl in return that told a story of poverty for him and the lack of his needed electronics.

Cookie sat back on her chaise lounge with

a drink in one hand and her *Town and Country* magazine in the other, sucking the stem of a maraschino cherry she'd just consumed. Her TV spot taping had gone splendidly, as usual, that jinx of a dog was back, and Craig was about to leave. It was, once again, a lush life.

"See ya!" she said to Craig's mopey back as he dragged the door open and plodded out.

Cranky Franky almost smiled in smug satisfaction. He'd be making a bundle on Saturday mating #63 with that stud from the fancy kennel. His beautiful, widely known and respected wife was the jewel in his crown, and soon he'd be bragging about his business exploits at the Kennelworth Club whilst tucking into a mound of his favorite steak tartar.

Life *was* but a dream. What they didn't know was that they would soon wake from their delirious reverie.

Chapter 12

The Plot Thickens

"Brambles, come quick!" Billy said urgently into his phone. "We've got a situation. OK, bring the dog, just come now!" Billy put the phone down in quiet desperation. In his mind, he'd done the right thing. He broke his own rule, caving in to the desires of his treasured family. He'd do it again, of course, but shouldn't his sacrifice have had a better outcome? He went out to the porch to await Brambles, his guru, while his family now sat with dull eyes, looking at nothing and responding to nothing he said.

Brambles knew and understood Billy's dog prohibition and had always honored it.

Still, he didn't feel he could leave his affectionate rescue, Nomad, home alone at this critical juncture. Nomad had only just arrived but had already rescued Brambles, who never admitted to his loneliness at his cottage. Nomad was his missing link. Thus, he'd agreed to come to the aid of his lovely niece and her vexed husband, but he'd refused to come without Nomad.

It was a dreadful scene Brambles encountered when he entered the family room of The Wishing Well. Hortense and the kids had exhausted their tears and were now inert on the couch. Billy paced, perplexed as never before. How could he get them out of this mess?

"So, as I understand it, Cranky, er, Francis, says she's his dog and came and got her," said Brambles, stroking his goatee in one hand and Nomad's head with the other as he assessed the situation. "Francis has always had a strong sense of ownership." Brambles and the Cruikshanks had once been partners in the car dealership until he came to his senses and walked away. Francis had blown a gasket when Brambles, the company's top salesperson, had the nerve to leave his company. *After all he'd done for Brambles!* Francis thought. It was the opposite, of course. Brambles had breathed new life into the fading dealership after Cookie's father, Fast Eddie Fagin, had died. Brambles knew that the best deals were made when everyone came out a winner, and he excelled at winning.

"So, they said she's chipped, so they can prove ownership," Brambles continued. "Hmmm. Bad sign. But one thing that I know about Cranky Franky Cruikshank is that he doesn't always tell the truth. Especially when the truth doesn't benefit him. If we could only get her over to Doc Booth to check her out. I'd go right over to Fagin's Resort to talk with the old buzzard, but I doubt that I'd be welcomed."

"But you used to be partners, Bram," Billy said. "Wouldn't he listen to you out of respect for all you did for the business?"

"He has no respect, and never did for anything, least of all himself. No, we'll have to tackle this another way," said Brambles, then continued to his niece and her children, "Don't you worry, we'll get her back, and you, Billy, will just have to live with it. There's plenty of room here for you to live separate but equal lives."

"Separate," said Hortense softly. "That would never work."

"Well, it'll have to, Hortense," said Billy. "I don't ask for much, but I'm firm on that!"

"Firm as Jell-O Jigglers," she retorted. "Do you know why you slept so well last night?"

"Yes, we were all exhausted, it was quiet, and there was a lovely cool breeze."

"Really? Just that?" Hortense was rarely disdainful.

"Of course, dearie, *and* sleeping with my sweetie pie."

"You always sleep with your sweetie pie, we're always exhausted, it's always quiet, there's always a cool breeze, and you still snore like a trumpet."

"Yes, I'm so sorry, dear, that nothing's worked. We could cuddle, and then I could sleep in the guest room."

"Nothing doing. There is a cure, however."

"What?"

"Wags."

"What?"

"Don't be dense, Billy. She's been sleeping under your chin, and when she does, you stop snoring and sleep well. And so do I! She's your cure, and now she's gone!"

"No way."

"Way. On her second day here, she climbed over the dog gate when we were all taking naps. I found her curled up under your chin, and you were breathing normally with a blissful smile on your face."

"No."

"Yes. I tested her healing powers again last night. After you'd gone to sleep, I smuggled Wags out from the family room and put her under your chin. Worked like magic. You were quiet as a church mouse. I smuggled her back out before you woke up. All night, she worked her magic on you. You were like two peas in a pod. Maybe she's so used to being hated, she naturally gravitated toward you."

"But she wasn't there, and besides, I hate dogs."

"I know you hate dogs, dearie, but she *was* with you, and both of us never slept better."

"I don't believe it!"

"Believe it. She rolled around in the yard last night and left a grass stain on your pillow."

"We'll see," said Billy, jumping to his feet and rushing upstairs to view the evidence.

"It wasn't me," Hortense called up after him. "I don't roll in the grass."

"But I'd have known if there was a dog in my bed," said Billy dejectedly, coming down the stairs and back into the family room with the grass-stained pillow in his hands.

"Darling, when you're snoring like a German Oom-Pah-Pah band, you wouldn't know it if an elephant crawled in bed with us, and there's no way an elephant would fit in this house to try that one out on you. It was funny," Hortense said with a giggle, "seeing you two characters cuddled up together like you were the best of friends."

"I just don't get it," said Billy.

"Just relax and let it sink in. You were meant for each other, dearie. Sometimes the truth hurts. By the way, you weren't the only one who had the best night's sleep in years. I slept like a bear in hibernation. It was marvelous sleeping with my honey and actually hearing the wind whistle through the trees outside and birdsongs in the morning."

"Really, darling?"

"Yes, my angel," Hortense said softly. "I've always loved you too much to complain about your snoring, but now that there's a cure . . . Wags is it! We *have* to get her back!" Turning to Brambles, she said, "You had the answer of what to do when we found her. Could you please help us find a way to get her back?"

"That's going to be more difficult, Hortense. I know those Cruikshanks well, and there's no love lost between us. We Wysywygs and Tiggywiggles have always lived on the premise that honesty is the best policy. Cranky Franky and Cookie live in another world with shifting rules and realities according to their own whims and perceived best interests. How can we help them understand that giving Wags back to us is in their best interest?"

"If it means keeping my family happy, I'll buy her back," said Billy, caving in to family pressure and his fear of disappointing them.

"It's worth a try," said Brambles, "but it may not be that easy."

Chapter 13

Assault on Fagin's Resort

Twilight was bathing Fagin's Resort in an auburn glow that almost made the place look inviting. Rarely had the atmosphere been so light and cheery. Getting Wags back was a twofer of benefits. Wags would be mated with Champion Sir Lancelot Lickalot of Lake Lucy, and the Cruikshanks got to stick it to those good-for-nothing, happy Tiggywiggles.

Who's happy now, thought Francis, with his eyes narrowed and lips tightened to a thin line slightly curving upward at the ends. He let out a self-satisfied grumble.

"Time for dinner, Francis," Cookie said.

They made their way to the garage. Francis gave her a nod and opened the door to the car for her with an uncharacteristically gentlemanly bow.

"I could get used to this," said Cookie. Francis's eyes widened with a start, and he slammed the door. He would never get used to being caring and polite for anyone, least of all his beautiful wife.

"Off we go in a flurry of horse turds, as Mom used to say!" said Cookie.

. . .

At The Wishing Well, the Tiggywiggles were conferring about Wags at their round kitchen table.

"I think it's too late to call with an offer," said Brambles. "They'll be off celebrating at the country club by now."

"Oh, dear," Hortense said. "A night without Wags . . ."

"You need your sleep, dearest," said her concerned husband. "I'll sleep on the couch in the living room."

"No, darling, I still love you too much for that."

"I'll try to snore softly then."

"You can't, my love, but I can't sleep with you, or without you."

"I'll ponder it," said Bram. Looking down at Nomad, who looked more worried than usual, he said, "We'll get your friend back."

Nomad was not as sanguine about their prospects. His head hung low, he leaned against Brambles and then slumped to the floor. What good was a cupboard full of Frenchy's Dog Food if his friend was in prison? He wanted to free all the residents of The Dogg House!

"What if she's not chipped?" Bea said hopefully.

"Yeah," Auggie said. "Wouldn't that mean that we could take her back?"

"I'm not sure," their uncle replied. "We'd have to get a hold of her and have her scanned. I doubt if the Cruikshanks would stand for that."

"Dear Brambles, you always have a way of turning lemons into lemonade, but this one has got you stumped," Hortense said.

"I'm afraid it does, Hortense. I'll call old Cranky Franky in the morning and offer him the moon and the stars."

"And a whole lot of money, if the moon and the stars are not enough," said Billy. His family all gasped in surprise as Billy now enthusiastically joined the reclamation party.

. . .

That night, nobody in the Tiggywiggle family slept well. Billy was either snoring like a basso profundo at the Metropolitan Opera or strategizing with Hortense, who took cat naps in between. The kids made a tent in Auggie's room with a blanket stretched over the two single beds. They hovered over a picture of Wags in the glimmer of their flashlights. Alternately, they cried and then seriously argued possible stratagems. Finally, they tossed back the blanket and set forth on their strongest maneuver. An assault on Fagin's Resort. Somehow, they'd bust her out!

With their flashlights in hand, they snuck

out of their home and walked, crouching, across Brambles' Sward like the paratroopers they saw on TV shows. Nomad barked as they passed their uncle's cottage, but quickly settled back down into his forlorn depression.

Summer foliage and a sky dark except for a faint crescent moon made it hard to find any of the trailheads, much less the right one. It took several tries. They were beginning to think they might have to spend the night there with the wild animals when they found the path to the Cruikshanks' compound. The twosome picked their way through the trees and bushes, stumbling here and there on fallen branches. It was spookier than Halloween. The eerie call of an owl made them jump in fright, but they didn't turn back. Their venture was too important.

Auggie and Bea breathed a communal sigh of relief when they came out of the woods relatively unscathed near the entrance to Fagin's Resort. Everything was dark and quiet. The Borzois, Ani and Vladi, couldn't be bothered with protecting anything but their toys and food bowls, so they were quiet. A faint howling sound in the wind added a spooky dimension. There was a large gated fence around the property. They could see a squawk box at the entrance, but they definitely didn't want to squawk, or make any noise at all. They couldn't go right up to the front door and demand their dog back, so they followed a driveway beyond the fence that made a wide arc around the house.

The driveway was gravel. To them, their footfalls sounded as loud as a Transformer's monstrous tramplings in an action movie. The drive took them into the dark, toward the outbuildings and kitchen gardens. The howling grew louder and spookier as they went on. As they got closer to a decrepit barn, a discordant choir of barking erupted from inside. Could they have put Wags in this broken-down firetrap? It couldn't be just Wags; it sounded like there was a multitude of voices, all in distress.

Frightened to their core, but determined to rescue Wags, they entered the leaning structure. In the light from a single bulb in a room toward the back, they could make out stacks of cages bursting with dogs. There were dozens of them. It was a puppy mill like the ones they had heard about but never imagined could exist in Endwell. They gasped.

One voice stood out as the one they were seeking: a shriek like a person who'd been bitten by a shark.

"Wags!" Auggie said in a stage whisper, not wanting to attract attention.

"There she is!" Bea exclaimed, quickly quieting her voice. They rushed over and found their beloved pup in a cage marked #63 that was secured with a huge, sturdy padlock. "Wags!" they whispered in joy.

Now what? They went back to the room with the light bulb to see if they could find the key. Wags's cage was the only one with a padlock; the other cages were just closed with hasps. There was a desk, four makeshift walls covered with photos of dogs with multicolored ribbons, and a wastebasket full of empty CheeZy Tots bags and cola cans. The desk produced little: some chewed-up pencils, a couple notepads from Fagin's Cars for the Stars, a few rumpled copies of *Doggo Delight* magazine, but nothing else. They used their flashlights to scour every inch of the space. They even used the rickety chair to explore the rafters, to no avail. They were angry, scared, tired, and couldn't think of what to do next.

"Maybe we could talk Craig into letting us take her to be scanned," Auggie said with a question in his tone.

"Maybe we could," said Bea. "All he cares about are his video games and money for electronics. He doesn't care about Wags."

"Still, he's as scared of his uncle as we are," said Auggie.

"The key to change . . . is to let go of fear," Bea recalled. "Remember? Uncle Brambles told us that Roseanne Cash, the singer, said that."

"All righty then, Iron Woman, let's go face our fears. Let's go right to the Cruikshanks themselves and knock on their door!" Auggie said like an army sergeant.

They rushed back to Wags's cage and tried to reassure her that they were going to spring her free, sticking their fingers through the wire mesh.

"Don't leave me here!" Wags yelped.

"We'll be back, Wags, and we'll free all of you," said Bea.

"Yeah," said Auggie in a worried tone. "Don't you worry!"

Their stomachs clenched, their shoulders tensed, and their breathing was shallow, but they soldiered on, walking out of the barn and back down the drive toward the squawk box at the front gate.

They stood back for a moment, considering their fate.

"What could go wrong?" said Auggie hopefully.

"Everything."

"Can you breathe?"

"Barely."

"Then let's give it a try before we pass out. Wags would do the same for us."

On tiptoes, they moved forward. About

ten feet from the gate, klieg lights snapped on and lit up the entire property all the way back to the dog barn. A loud whistling sound *whup, whup, whupped*, and a robotic voice from an overhead speaker issued commands.

"Do not approach this property. Stand back. Repeat. Do not approach this property. Stand back. Do not approach this property. Stand back. Repeat. Stand back."

They obeyed, and the voice stopped. The outdoor lights stayed on.

Lights came on in the house, and they could see movement of people through the windows. What would their parents say if they learned their kids had made an assault on their neighbors' house? Without consulting each other, they turned their backs to Fagin's Resort and ran toward the woods, dropping their flashlights along the way. They crashed into the brush, hoping they'd find the trail, scrambling over all sorts of natural obstacles until they came out on the other side.

. . .

"Uncle Brambles!"

"Help!"

In their terror, they pounded on his door, not caring that it was the middle of the night.

Nomad began to bark, and Brambles arose from his restless slumber. He hobbled downstairs and opened the door to two frightened faces.

"What have we got here?" said Brambles. Nomad came out and greeted the kids with wags and kisses and then herded them into the cottage.

"We tried to bust Wags out of the Cruikshanks' barn," Bea said breathlessly.

"She's locked up in a cage, and we couldn't find the key," said Auggie.

"There are dozens of cages with dogs in 'em stacked up in the barn!" said Bea.

"It's really nasty too, Uncle Brambles," said Auggie. "The cages were dirty and smelly. Poor Wags!"

"She shouldn't be in there," said Bea. "None of them should be there!"

"It's just cruel," said Auggie.

"You're right—both of you. Sounds like Francis and Cookie have a puppy mill. I shouldn't be surprised, but still, it's a shock knowing that there are people who treat animals that way. You better come in the kitchen. This situation calls for lemonade and Girl Scout cookies. I still have a box in the pantry."

They went into the kitchen, and Brambles poured the lemonade while the kids found the cookies in the pantry and opened them up. They sat together at the table, not touching their snacks. Nomad took a seat on Brambles's lap as the three humans conferred.

"First, we have to call your parents. They'll be beside themselves if they find you missing, and while they're on the way over, you can tell me what happened."

Brambles called Hortense and Billy, who, though not really sleeping, were barely conscious. After they expressed shock, dismay, and anger at their kids for running off without their permission, Brambles suggested they take their time with coming over to collect them to give him some time to extract the whole story. They agreed.

At The Wishing Well, Hortense said to Billy, "You see, we *have* to get her back. It's splintering our family."

"You're right, dear rose petal, you're right."

"Our kids would never have run away for any other reason."

"Yes, we'll have to fix this. I just hope money will be the answer."

"It better be. We've got to get her back. NOW!"

They sprung out of bed, grabbed their robes, and rushed to the lodge while Brambles pieced together the scenario as the children spoke in torrents, often at the same time.

. . .

When their parents arrived, the children were sipping their lemonade and munching on cookies.

"Bea! Auggie! How could you? You nearly scared us to death!" Hortense exclaimed, rushing into Brambles's kitchen with Billy. She knelt on the floor between the children and wrapped her arms around them.

"You can have the dog, honestly, but just don't go trespassing on the Cruikshanks' property. They have shotguns and very bad tempers," Billy implored. "We love you! To the moon . . ."

"And back," Hortense finished.

"I'll call Francis in the morning at the office where he can't make too much of a fuss," said Brambles. "In the meantime, no more sub-military actions, you two. You hear? You'll give your parents heart attacks."

Brambles fortified the lemonade with adult beverages for Hortense and Billy. As the drinks worked their magic, the feelings of fright all around eased up. They were all relieved to have survived a near catastrophe. But Wags was still incarcerated at the puppy mill. That was another problem. Brambles, a former lawyer and car dealer, explained that puppy mills were not illegal in the state of

Wisconsin, but they weren't well thought of, and animal cruelty *was* against the law.

Now, they had dozens more dogs to rescue in addition to Wags. Beaten from every angle, Billy caved, saying that they could harbor the dogs at The Wishing Well until they could find homes for them. Brambles strategized a plan to turn the garages into temporary shelters and reach out to the local rescue organizations, Doggo-Rama and Dog On It, to arrange foster homes. The whole thing turned Billy's world upside down. After his firm "no dog" policy, now Brambles was suggesting a way to shelter dozens of dogs at The Wishing Well!

How could this have happened to him? Hortense was not unaware of the flexibility Billy was showing and how his love for his family and their happiness was more important than anything else to him. She reached across the table and put her hand warmly on top of his. Their eyes met in perfect understanding.

Though not at all sure themselves, the

adults assured the children they would get Wags back. The kids knew they were just saying it for their sake but tried to act as though they believed it and had faith in them. With nothing else to do that evening, they returned to their beds at home. Sleep, however, was nothing but a dream.

. . .

Anger and indignation filled the air at Fagin's Resort. Lights were ablaze on the entire property. Francis rushed out to The Dogg House in his undershorts with Vladi to make sure the dogs, especially Wags, were all there. They were, but it was clear from an overturned chair and papers strewn around the floor that someone had been in the office looking for something. Cookie, in her flowing pink nightgown and furry, high-heeled mules, tottered out into the yard with Ani to see what had set off the alarm. All she found were a couple of flashlights at the edge of the woods.

She met Francis back at the house.

"It was those Tiggywiggles! I'm sure of it!" Cookie hissed.

Her husband was seething with anger, his brow deeply furrowed and his lips curved downward in a frightening scowl. Trespassing was illegal, but calling the police might not be their best move. The Endwell police chief, Dimonte Deck, was a known animal lover and chairman of the board of the Dog On It rescue organization. He took his drug-sniffing chihuahua, Sarge, who'd been rescued from a drug house sting, everywhere with him. If they called the police, the property would be scoured, The Dogg House would be discovered, and then *they'd* be in the doghouse.

Francis agreed with Cookie. It was the Tiggywiggles. He knew it even if he couldn't prove it. Somehow, he would get back at those Tiggywiggles. He'd make them pay.

"Hortense and Billy wouldn't dare trespass on our property, so it had to be those obnoxious kids. They're always such a lovely-dovey family," Cookie said resentfully. "This is the last of them. This will tear them apart. Billy never wanted a dog, and I'll see to it that he'll never get #63! Just let them try to keep us from mating her with Sir Lickalot. They haven't got a chance. She's ours, and we'll never let her go!"

. . .

The Tiggywiggles reconvened the next morning at the breakfast table, red-eyed and worn to a frazzle. Their confidence beaten, none of them were up to cooking, so Hortense got out boxes of cereal. She filled their bowls, poured oat milk on them, and passed them out. None of them had any appetite. The cereal got soggy as they distractedly stirred it around in their bowls.

"Bram'll talk to them. It'll all work out," said Hortense, although she didn't see how it could. The wall of meanness on the part of the Cruikshanks was hard to overcome.

. . .

Not having slept much, Brambles got up early and took Nomad for a walk in the woods to the edge of Fagin's Resort, but not close enough to set off the alarms. As he gazed at the mansion, he wondered what he had that they could possibly want. He'd give them anything to free Wags and all the other dogs.

He and Nomad roamed several trails, putting off returning home to make the inevitable call to Francis. Though he was normally self-confident, Brambles shuttered at the prospect of calling his ex-partner, who had something he very much wanted: Wags.

Back at home, Brambles made the call.

"No need to shout, Francis," said Brambles into the phone. "They can probably hear you down to the Dandy Diner. Yes, it was our kids, but they meant no harm, they just want their dog back. Take a deep, slow breath, Francis. At this rate you'll have a heart attack and you won't be able to worry about a little dog. The kids want to apologize and get Wags back home where she belongs. Yes, I guess that would be #63. We'll buy her from you. Name your price."

"Well, that's not very nice at all," said Brambles into the phone that had exploded with vituperative noise and then abruptly was slammed shut. *That didn't go well,* he thought. Brambles was extremely resourceful, but even he was running out of tricks. He was too distracted to sculpt, cook, or even make a pot of coffee. Needing sustenance and good company, he left for the Dandy Diner, leaving Nomad with a bone to chew on while he was away.

Chapter 14

The Mating Game

"Hey, hey, good lookin'! I got breakfast cookin'. How 'bout I cook some up for you?" Finessa Bopp said to her favorite customer, Brambles Wysywyg. She was the chef/owner of Endwell's most popular eatery, The Dandy Diner. "Really, though, Brambles, I've never, ever had to say this to you before, but you look awful!"

Brambles hadn't changed from his overalls that he'd donned, thinking he'd work off some steam by molding his sculpture of Nomad. He'd forgotten to comb his hair, and his nails were filled with red clay. This was an unusual presentation for the normally dapper artist, who took a seat at the counter.

"Just coffee," said Brambles, barely remembering to add his customary, "Thank you."

"You look like you could use the hair of the dog that bit you more than a cup of coffee."

"Pour the coffee, Finessa. Regular, extra cream, two sugars. The usual, although nothing is usual today. I don't want the hair of the dog that bit me, I want the whole dog."

"I don't get it."

"Last Sunday, Bea and Auggie found a stray dog at Woofstock . . ."

"Yeah, I remember, they were showing her picture around the fairgrounds that afternoon. They didn't take him home, did they?"

"Yes, they did. It's a miracle, Finessa. Billy said they could keep her in the family room until we found her family."

"Well, that *is* amazing, and good so far, isn't it?"

"No, because we all—*including* Billy—have fallen in love with her *and* we've found her family."

"That's rough. I'm sorry for the kids especially. Life sometimes gives you mountains, and the kids'll have to learn how to climb them."

"That's just what they tried to do. They went to the family's home and tried to get her back."

"They are good kids, always nice and respectful."

"Nice and respectful, but they trespassed on my neighbor's property, and now he's enraged."

"They're just kids. Just childhood mischief, anyway. He'll get over it. Any chance you could buy the dog off him for the kids? Win-win. All around."

"It's the Cruikshanks, Finessa."

"Oh my," said Finessa. She stumbled backward, about to collapse from the shock. With the coffee carafe in her hand, she staggered around the counter and took the seat next to Brambles. She set the carafe down and took a deep breath as Brambles began to speak.

"I already called Francis and told him to name his price. They have her locked up in a cage in their barn, but they won't give her up. They're expecting to make a mint using her as a breeding dog."

"It ain't right. It just ain't right," she said, sighing deeply. "How can I help? Breakfast is on me, and don't you argue with me, Brambles Wysywyg! *And* don't tell me you're not hungry. You'll need a good meal to get you through this. This is something even you can't handle alone. I'm calling Faith. She'll know what to do."

"Why Faith?"

"She knows more about dogs than Dr. Booth, with no disrespect to our vet. She also knows every dog in town."

"She may have missed a few …" said Brambles.

Finessa gave him a questioning look.

"The Cruikshanks are running a puppy mill on their property."

"Well, that's it, then. Have *them* arrested before they can bring charges against those innocent children."

"Dear Finessa, as repugnant as they are,

puppy mills are not illegal, so there's no way to shut them down."

"Have faith, and have your breakfast."

Finessa returned to her grill and started to brown a pile of hash browns. As the bacon was crisping at the back of the cooktop, she made a quick call. Then she expertly dropped a couple eggs on the griddle, covered them with a pot lid, and let them sizzle until they were perfectly sunny-side up. She added a layer of chopped onions onto the hash browns and loaded Brambles's plate, handing him a squeeze bottle with her own green tomatillo salsa.

"Eat," she ordered, putting the plate down in front of him. "This won't be an easy battle."

Finessa's breakfasts were the best Brambles had ever tasted, including the ones he used to enjoy at the fancy restaurants he frequented when he was a successful car dealer. Even his own mother's didn't compare to Finessa's. He hadn't thought that he could eat, but the aroma of the food steaming up into his nostrils was impossible to resist. He picked up his fork and dug in. When he was almost finished, Finessa came over to refill his cup of coffee. With a *whoosh*, the door opened, and a woman wearing glittering cat-eye sunglasses and a summer dress printed with chihuahuas all over it and carrying a dachshund-shaped purse, rushed in.

"How ya doin', old buddy?" said Faith, owner of the Au Naturel Pet Store, taking a seat next to Brambles.

"Not old," said Brambles, chewing the last piece of toast. He swallowed and said, "Old buddy, yourself."

"I can't stay long," said Faith. "Patience is running the store for me. She means well, but it takes a lot of patience to work with her. She's just young—she'll get it, eventually. Finessa said you have an emergency."

Finessa put a cup of coffee in front of Faith and filled it, pushing the creamer and sugar closer to her. Faith took a moment to doctor her coffee and think. In a low voice, she said, "It's the Cruikshanks."

"Yes," said Brambles.

"They have that dog the kids found?"

"Yes. I offered to buy her, but they refused."

"Naturally, they know you want her, and they hate you and your family. They loathe your happiness."

"It's OK, Faith. It was nice of you to come over, but I know there's nothing . . ."

"Whoa! Hold up there, cowboy. Who said there's nothing we can do? I've got a couple of aces up my sleeve and plan to use them." She leaned into Brambles and, talking in hushed tones, came up with a plan. And it was a good one.

. . .

At The Wishing Well, the kids were lolling around the porch, trying to get into their computer games. Hortense and Billy sat together in the kitchen. Hortense said quietly to Billy, "There's really nothing Cranky Franky can do to the kids. Puppy mills aren't illegal, but they'd have a hard time defending themselves in the court of popular opinion.

Let's all take a day off and go to the beach. It's warm enough to swim, so we can work off some of this angst. We'll all think more clearly after a break. If those Cruikshanks decide to call the police on the kids, we won't be here to be served the papers."

"You're right, as always, my angel," said Billy. "You always know just what to do. I guess you learned that from Brambles."

Hortense whispered into Billy's ear, "I expect so, but I'm not any closer to getting Wags back. This'll be a time for us to rest and recuperate before the next skirmish."

"Kids!" Billy called out. "Mom and I are going to take you to the beach. How's that?"

The kids murmured their unenthusiastic approval.

"Come on, gang!" Billy said, hoping to lift the dark mood they all shared. "How about some banana split sundaes at Ice Queen's Ice Cream?"

"Before lunch?" said Bea. Even the kids were surprised.

"Endorphins, honey bunches of groats.

Endorphins! Tough times, tough measures. I think I'll have extra pecans on mine."

They drove into Milwaukee to the classic custard stand, where a number of Presidents had enjoyed their rich and creamy custard. After their restorative sundaes, they headed for Kohler-Andrae State Park on Lake Michigan. They spent hours climbing the massive sand dunes and then cooling off in the brisk lake waters. Together, with mounting confidence and cheer, they sang "You Ain't Nothin' But A Hound Dog." It was Billy's favorite song.

Chapter 15

Lickalot's Dilemma

At The Dogg House, Wags was once again aggravated and aggrieved, fuming in cage #63.

"Of course, we all missed you, Wags, but we're not glad you're back," said Kind Kirby from a cage one row up and two cages over. "We all hoped that you'd gotten free forever. That's a dream we all share." The mood at The Dogg House was somber and defeated. If Wags couldn't make it out for good, they all wondered if there was any hope for themselves.

"I missed you too, Kirby. I was hoping there was some way I could spring the whole lot of us. It was a good dream, anyway," said

Wags angrily. Now, she thought she might not even have visits from Nomad since he had a home of his own. Still, she wasn't jealous of his good fortune. *He's a good soul who deserves a good home,* she thought. "At least Nomad found a home," she said aloud to the barnful of lost souls.

They all howled a sorrowful song.

On the other hand, the mood at Fagin's Resort was almost cheery, if that were possible in the gloomy mansion. Cookie was in the kitchen writing copy for her next commercial: "At Fagin's Cars for the Stars, Everyone's a Star!" It was good, she thought. Maybe she could corral some kids to say, "You're a Star," in baby talk. A pizza party for all the kids ought to do it, and it would be well worth the expense.

Francis was going over accounts in his office, which was thick with cigar smoke the way he liked it. He loved to look at the balance sheet when it was balanced in his favor. He would've loved to have stacks of paper money to sort and pile, but his computerized ledger was almost as good. Maybe he *would* take Cookie on the scuba diving trip to Pulao. He wouldn't mind showing off his beautiful wife, the hotel would be air-conditioned, and he could Zoom his accountant for regular updates on his money situation.

The Dogg House had turned into a major revenue source for the Cruikshanks, who made six figures a year selling their puppies. Mating Wags was just for fun money. It was small potatoes in the scheme of finances for Cruikshank, but Francis liked money wherever it came from, and this was a great way to stick it to the Tiggywiggles. They had no idea how much he hated them for their happiness and how deviously he'd scheme to destroy it.

. . .

Craig was at home with his parents and their cats, watching the Shop 'Til You Drop network on TV. Two women were showing off what they described as "one-of-a-kind purple topaz rings" for a price they said would never be duplicated. His mother, not a computer wizard, was on the phone, anxiously awaiting the customer service representative to take her order before they ran out of the "one-of-a-kind" item. She had dozens of boxes of jewelry from STYD in her closet, unopened, awaiting the perfect occasion to wear them.

Craig wondered if he'd ever achieve the level of his game that he was on when the trouble started. He'd implored his parents for the money to replace his laptop, but they said they couldn't help. They had cats to feed and STYD bills to pay, and Craig's father's income as the maintenance man at Fagin's Cars for the Stars didn't stretch that far.

How could his uncle have reneged on his payment for watching The Dogg House? Craig was steamed. And worse, how could Uncle Francis not replace Craig's laptop when it was *his* dog that broke it? The injustice of it all made Craig almost want to do something about it. Instead, he got a CapiCola and a large bag of CheeZy Tots from the kitchen and plopped into a comfortable armchair in front of the TV. In an instant, he was buried in cats mewling and kneading his arms with their claws. Craig hated animals. All animals, including the human variety, especially Uncle Francis and his bogus wife, Cookie.

. . .

Champion Sir Lancelot Lickalot of Lake Lucy was in such hot demand that his human, Lydia Déjeuner, charged a $1,000 stud fee up front with a no-money-back policy if the breeding didn't take. As stingy as Francis Cruikshank was, Sir Lancelot's reputation as a stud dog sold him on the deal. Sir Lickalot's championship heritage went back generations, and his offspring brought huge prices, as they were all title holders in the dog show circuit. Francis expected a huge percentage return on his investment, better than anything he could make on the stock market.

. . .

Brambles was still conferring with Faith and Finessa at The Dandy Diner. Faith never liked the haughty Cruikshanks, even though they were regular customers. She always sensed that there was something shady about them, although she couldn't put her finger on it. When Bram told her that they were operating a secret puppy mill, she wanted to help in any way she could.

. . .

Craig's parents were paupers who aspired to wealth. Brambles had sold them their beige 2005 Cadillac DeVille when he was still a car dealer. He understood their poverty and pretentions, but would never stoop to shaming them. Instead, he found them a "Granny" car, a vehicle in mint condition that had barely been driven by its elderly owner. He never breathed a word that they hadn't bought the car new at full price. Bram let them have their fantasies, and they somewhat grudgingly appreciated him for it.

They were very concerned about Craig's falling out with the wealthy branch of the family, Francis and Cookie, and were angry with them for not paying Craig his due. When Brambles called them with an idea of how to get back at the crooked Cruikshanks, they jumped at the chance.

. . .

"Craig!" Mrs. Cruikshank shouted over the blaring TV and cat purring. "Get over to your uncle's and offer to clean up the cages at The Dogg House and feed the dogs!" The boy remained unmoved by his mother's supplications until she stabbed him in the ribs with a cat toy. He was too depressed to do anything but eat and zone out to the droning tone of the TV, but his mother would not let him rest. Finally, he shrugged off the abundant cat population around his neck and torso, got up, and followed his mother's orders.

"Here," she said, shoving a foil packet with a pill wrapped in a wad of Kunstler's

Braunschweiger in his hand as he left the house. "Give this to that dog that broke your computer. It'll serve that old Cranky Franky right."

. . .

Now *he* was aggravated and aggrieved. As he trudged over to his uncle's house, Craig observed, with both admiration and resentment, how the butterflies sailed so freely on the pleasant gusts of wind that ruffled his hair. How he wished he could join them, flitting here and there, sampling the nectar of late-summer flowers, carefree like he would like to be.

When Craig arrived at Fagin's Resort and offered his services, Francis and Cookie acted as though they'd expected him and he was simply carrying out his unpaid duties as expected. "Your highnesses," he sneered under his breath. He had no intention of cleaning up the dog cages, but schlepped back to the kennels with his potion for Wags. Craig didn't know what it was and didn't care. He just hoped that it would make her sick, or worse.

He unwrapped the Braunschweiger-encased pill, thinking it smelled good and hoped there was enough left of the undoctored sausage for a jumbo sammy when he got home. He administered the pill as directed by his mom, who'd been directed by Brambles, who'd been directed by Faith. Hungry after a couple of days back in the bleak world of The Dogg House, Wags snarfed it down immediately when Craig pushed it through the wire mesh of her cage on a stick from the yard, fearing she'd bite his fingers off if he got any closer.

The pill contained a powerful dose of chlorophyll. Though non-toxic to Wags, it would create a scent so foul to Champion Sir Lancelot Lickalot, it would put him off from mating. Even though he was the premier Casanova in the Yorkie breeding world, he would be disgusted by Wags with her minty-fresh aroma.

Mission accomplished, Craig slunk back

to his electronics-free lair at home for his only compensation, a luscious "Milwaukee Heart Attack Sandwich" of liver sausage with raw onions and dark mustard on dark caraway rye bread.

. . .

Late that afternoon, the Tiggywiggles returned, rejuvenated from their day at the beach. They were all more cheerful when they returned home, although nothing had really changed. Nothing that they knew of. Brambles was not about to spill the beans, not knowing if Faith's strategy would really work.

. . .

On Saturday morning, Wags awoke to the howls of The Dogg House regulars. According to Francis's calculations, the timing was perfect to mate her with Champion Sir Lancelot Lickalot of Lake Lucy. Cookie had designed a luxurious mating pen festooned with flags and lined with a red silk mattress to make it look like a castle. It was just what she thought the champion would expect.

"You don't smell so good," said Kind Kirby to Wags, sniffing in her direction.

"I'll have you know, I call my scent 'Eau de Stinky Roll,'" she retorted, highly offended by the accusation.

"I mean, you don't smell much at all. If anything, you have a rather disgustingly piney odor. Weird. You normally stink in a good way like the rest of us," he said in an ameliorating tone, simply noting the realities of kennel life with baths only for the pups for sale.

"Kind Kirby, I've never known you to be so cruel!" said Wags in a huff, turning her head away.

That knuckleheaded human, Craig, at his uncle's command, was hovering in the background, not knowing what to do with himself with no computer for entertainment. He could've cleaned out the cages, refilled the water bowls, and fed the dogs, but he was just too depressed about the whole situation to do anything. He sluffed off to the chair in the office, tilted it back with his feet on the desk, and tried to rock away the tension he felt.

Lydia Déjeuner arrived midmorning with Sir Lancelot Lickalot. She opened the door of her Escalade and pulled out a red-carpeted ramp for the regal canine to descend. He was dressed in a purple silk jacket with a white fur collar despite the late-summer warmth. It was his mating outfit. He wouldn't consider the proposition without the proper pomp and circumstance accorded to a monarch of his realm. Francis wore a smug grin as the regal pooch trotted out into the yard. Cookie oohed and ahhed at his magnificence, whilst Licky lifted his leg on Francis's expensive, brown Allen Edmonds cordovan shoes. Craig, who'd come to the door of the barn to observe the scene, barely contained his laugher.

"EEE . . ." Francis was about to let out a scream when Cookie stopped him, grabbing his arm and giving him a look that reminded him that he'd be able to replace the pricey shoes a dozen times over if all went well today.

"Isn't he just a doll," Cookie said admiringly. "We have a mating pen in the barn all decked out for the occasion."

"The barn?" Déjeuner sniffed. Really, it was too vulgar. But reality bites sometimes. She needed the $1,000 cash infusion to bolster her pyramid marketing scheme of selling gourmet meals on edible trays for dogs. She held out her hands to Francis, who filled them with cash. She spent the next few tension-filled minutes carefully counting it.

"It's all there!" said Cookie cheerily.

Déjeuner huffed her frustration, nearly losing her count. When she determined the amount was correct, she stashed the cash in a lockbox in the Escalade and followed the Cruikshanks into the barn. There was little to disguise the place as a puppy mill, but Déjeuner wasn't about to report it. Once Sir Lickalot had done his duty, they'd be off to deposit their loot in the bank and have lunch at Oscar's Hot Dog Hamlet, an exclusive restaurant that catered only to the best of pups and humans.

As Francis yanked Wags out of cage #63, she snarled furiously, bit his thumb, and dashed away from him, hoping to regain her freedom. Unfortunately, Cookie was standing right behind her husband. She snatched Wags up with her long, pink nails extended on her lengthy fingers. *Curses*, thought Wags. *Foiled again!*

"She's such a spirited little dog. A perfect temperament, really. After all, you don't want a dog who's a pushover," Cookie said.

Déjeuner narrowed her eyes, looking at Sir Lickalot's consort. Cookie had hired a mobile groomer to come out and beautify Wags for her mating. Still, she still had a few scraggy dreadlocks around her face that the groomer couldn't remove without shaving her completely, leaving her to look a little more like a rat with a big nose than a champion Yorkie.

"Here she is, our little love," said Cookie, pushing a rumbling Wags into the mating pen.

"You sure you've got her rabies up to date?" said Déjeuner doubtfully.

"Not to worry, Ms. Déjeuner, she's up to date and ready to mate!" Cookie responded, giggling at her own perfect rhyme.

Déjeuner picked up Licky and put him in the pen near Wags. "Where is she?" he asked, looking indignantly up toward his human as Wags scuttled over to the far corner of the pen. Champion Sir Lancelot Lickalot sniffed in her direction. Nothing. He turned his nose up in the air and sniffed all around. Nothing. With her matted dreadlocks, Sir Lickalot thought she looked appalling. Worse yet, Wags didn't *smell* attractive. In fact, she had little smell at all except for a faint aroma of toothpaste that did not arouse him. The chlorophyll capsule was working its magic! Sir Lickalot crinkled his nose in disdain at Wags and gave his human the stink eye. What depths of degradation could he be subjected to now? He was deeply offended. He dropped down on all fours at the opposite side of the pen and rolled on his side in unspeakable boredom at the whole affair.

Cookie said, "He's criminally cute, Ms.

Déjeuner. Look how he's warming up to #63!" She bent over the enclosure, hiding Wags while she dipped into a treat pouch for a fingerful of Kunstler's Braunschweiger, which she spread inside Wag's collar. "Now she's ready," Cookie said, pretending to have given Wags encouraging affection. She hated the dog!

Sir Lickalot perked up at the aroma of Braunschweiger. *Now you're talking*, he thought. He followed the scent right to Wags, the reprobate, in the corner and made a lunge for her neck. "Gotcha!" he said to Wags, pulling the collar right off her neck and taking it back to his corner of the pen. He licked and chewed it lustily, a lust the humans had hoped would join the dogs in holy matrimony. Wags bared her teeth, looking in Lickalot's direction. He was too busy to notice.

"Let's have coffee on the lanai and leave them to do their business," said Cookie undauntedly to Ms. Déjeuner.

"Let's not!" was Déjeuner's retort. "Gimme the collar, Licky," she said, pulling the delectable item out of his jaws. She shoved the moist, shredded collar into Cookie's hands, picked up Licky, and marched toward her car.

"What about our $1,000 dollars?" Cookie implored to Déjeuner's back.

"What about it?" said Déjeuner without turning around. "A thousand bucks up front. No guarantee. That was the deal!" She was putting Sir Licky in his fur-lined car seat when she heard Cranky Franky Cruikshank explode.

"Get rid of her!" he bellowed to Craig, who'd been lollygagging around the fringes of the affair. "Get her out of my sight!" he said as though his words were epithets.

Startled by his ferocity, Déjeuner jumped into her car and buckled up. She pressed down hard on the gas pedal, turned the steering wheel sharply, and issued a spray of gravel in her wake.

Cookie was shocked. Francis was as red as the famous Wisconsin Door County sour cherries he so loved in pies.

Chapter 16

Get Rid of Her!

"Take her," Cookie said to Craig, picking up Wags and shoving her into his arms. With that, she grabbed her husband's arm and dragged him toward the bar on the lanai. She thought she could douse a bit of her cranky husband's rage and turn his attention to something more cheerful, like the pictures of her Pulao paradise from the magazine.

. . .

Craig stood, his mouth agape, with the pooch who'd started the whole mess in his arms. He was puzzled. Did they really mean

for him to *get rid* of her? He could extin-
guish dozens of oncoming assailants in his
video games without thinking, but *get rid*
of a live animal? For real? "You got it, Aunt
Cookie, Uncle Francis!" he called after them.
In an uncharacteristic show of emotion, when
they'd closed the door behind them, Craig
whispered angrily, "I'll do just what you say,
exactly the way you would do it yourselves!"

. . .

The day at the beach had reduced the
stress levels at The Wishing Well. Saturday
morning, Billy and the kids were refreshed
and ready for the next challenge. Hortense
hadn't slept well with Billy snorting all night
at high volume. She felt rather groggy and
disoriented. They had to continue their ef-
forts to get Wags back, and they could use all
the help they could get, so Hortense asked
Billy to call Brambles.

"Oh, for Pete's sake, Brambles," Billy exhaled into the phone. "Next thing you know,

we'll be an animal shelter. Sure thing, Bram, of course, bring Nomad along." His children cheered in the background.

Brambles, of course, was harboring the secret of the strategy he'd developed with Faith and Finessa. He longed to tell the Tiggywiggles about it, but didn't dare for fear of getting their hopes up, perhaps to be dashed asunder if it failed.

Faith had suggested the chlorophyll capsule to mask Wags's true doggy scent and make her undesirable to Champion Sir Lancelot Lickalot of Lake Lucy. She was familiar with Licky because his human, Lydia Déjeuner, brought him along when she shopped at her store to buy pheromone capsules to calm him before shows.

Like many pet owners in Endwell, Déjeuner bought her dog food from Faith because it was non-GMO, gluten free, and, well, it was nearly food free. Licky was rather wishy-washy about food. He was tired of the homemade chicken and rice with carrot medallions that Lydia made for him. Often, he'd sit next to his bowl with his legs splayed to one side and just sigh in silent desperation. He didn't care if the other dogs in the house stole his food. *Let 'em have it*, he thought. Faith knew that the one thing he couldn't resist was Kunstler's Braunschweiger. He'd wrestle a muscle-bound American Staffordshire Terrier to the death for a thimbleful of the savory sausage. Of course, Faith didn't share that information with Cookie.

By now, Brambles was dying to know if the chlorophyll had worked, but couldn't exactly call up his old partner, Francis, to find out. Earlier that morning, over coffee at The Dandy Diner, he and Finessa Bopp had reviewed every possible scenario, none of which were terribly reassuring. He and Nomad were both restless and welcomed the call from Billy that necessitated a nice walk over to The Wishing Well.

He brought a small box of Finessa's amazing Italian cookies to fortify the forces. While the Tiggywiggles were heatedly comparing the advantages of frosted chocolate tutus over pignoli cookies with toasted pine nuts, a call came in to Brambles's phone. It was Faith. Brambles, who'd never interrupted a conversation to take a call on his cell phone, said, "I've got to take this," then ducked into the family room off the kitchen for privacy.

"What happened?" he demanded of his colleague in crime. "Did it work?"

Faith, talking quietly to keep customers from overhearing their conversation, said tentatively, "I think so. Lydia was just in with Licky, and she bought an extra supply of pheromones. She said that the mating was a bust. Licky didn't go for Wags until the end, and then he just grabbed her collar and chewed it to bits."

"He was attracted to her collar, but not her? Right?" Brambles inquired with a self-satisfied smile.

"Right, and Cranky Franky was livid. He told that lazy nephew of his to get rid of her!"

"What? Wags? No! That can't be!" Brambles was aghast. "Where is she now?"

"Dunno. That's all Lydia told me. Doesn't

look good for Wags, though. Sorry, Bram. I really am, but I've got customers. I've got to go."

"Yes, of course, Faith. Thank you. Really, you were a great help. It was a terrific idea . . ." Brambles said dispiritedly. He wondered what that meathead nephew would do with her. "Now what?" he said aloud to himself.

Returning to the kitchen, Brambles could no longer keep the secret. He told his family about his plans, the execution, the initial success, and finally, the resounding failure of his mission.

"What'll Craig do with her?" asked Bea, shivering with fear.

"He wouldn't really hurt her, would he?" said Auggie in a panicked voice.

"We've got to get out and find her, pronto!" said Hortense. "Kids, you and Brambles take Nomad and look for her in the woods. Billy, you and I can go in the Range Rover and scour the town." Hortense delivered her orders with military precision. Her troops were setting off on their missions when Billy said, "Someone's got to hold down the fort. Hortense, you stay here, and we'll scour Endwell top to bottom."

"OK," she agreed without conviction. *Now what?* she thought. *Make a frontal assault on Fagin's Resort?* She hoped it wouldn't come to that.

. . .

Craig Cruikshank had never had, nor wanted, a dog. He wasn't enthralled with his family's legions of cats either. He preferred the virtual world of combat and victory. Until now, he'd spent most of his time playing video games, and his life had buzzed along with minimal complications. Now, he had a dog he didn't like in his arms with the orders to "get rid of her" from his uncle. Uncle Francis had played a major role in funding his video exploits, not because of his generosity, but through employing Craig at The Dogg House.

Ever since Dog #63 ran away, however, that revenue source had dried up. Since his stingy uncle had refused to pay him for his weekend monitoring The Dogg House during Woofstock, it seemed unlikely that his uncle would pay him for anything else in the future. Craig had been left high and dry with a despicable task that he didn't want to do and wouldn't get paid for. Shoot! He was tired of his uncle taking advantage of him! So, what was the worst thing he could do with this wretched pooch? He considered his options and came up with an idea. *Old Cranky Franky will love this one! Not!* he thought as Wags struggled in his arms to get free.

. . .

Nomad was worried about Wags. He knew that she was resourceful, but he didn't see how even she could get out of this mess. She had received what sounded like a death sentence from the worst of humankind: Francis Cruikshank. Nomad had not had much luck with humans prior to moving in with Brambles, and once again, he was concerned about his friend's well-being in the hands of such un-savory humans. He was glad to play a role in rescuing Wags. He and Brambles knew the woods like nobody else.

As Nomad, Brambles, Bea, and Auggie approached the entrance to the woods, No-mad held his nose high to capture Wags's scent. Nothing. That was odd. She should've left some kind of aroma to follow.

"He's trying to sniff her out, and he can't pick up her scent," said Brambles. "We should never have given her those chlorophyll cap-sules!"

"You were trying to help, Uncle Brambles," Bea said comfortingly.

"We'll find her," said Auggie with a ques-tion in his tone.

"Yes, we will," Brambles said firmly. "You're right, Auggie. We've got to keep a positive at-titude. Yes, we will find her. Nomad, lead the way!"

Without her scent to guide him, Nomad directed his search party to a path that came out at Fagin's Resort, where this nightmare had begun. Maybe Kind Kirby would know where she went. He hoped so.

. . .

Billy approached his task methodically, starting with a visit to Faith at the Au Naturel Pet Store.

"We've got to find her, Faith," Billy implored. "She's cured my snoring! For the first time since our wedding, Hortense is getting a full night's sleep. We've just got to get her back before Craig gets rid of her like his uncle demanded."

"I'll put out a Facebook APB with our Doggo-Rama, Dog On It and ASPizzaCA chapters. I'll have my customers go on the lookout too. We'll get her back, don't you worry, Billy," she said in a voice that conveyed her very deep worry.

Billy then stopped at The Dandy Diner to check in with Chef Bopp. He knew she was an avid agility competitor with her dog, Monty. He'd barely opened the door when she called out to him, "We're on it, Billy! We'll get your dog back." They'd not had time to make flyers, but Billy had Wags's pictures on his phone, if needed. The town of Endwell seemed to want this escapade to end well for Wags and the Tiggywiggles.

Chapter 17

Craig's Dilemma

"You're a real Tiggywiggle, you little squirt!" Craig said to the Yorkie struggling in his arms. "You wiggle more than Jell-O Jigglers." Walking out of Fagin's Resort on the main drive, he missed Brambles's search party that was rooting around in the woods. Billy had driven away from The Wishing Well toward town, so he didn't see Craig with Wags tucked tightly under his arm as they came out on Lilac Lane. It was a lovely late-summer day: sunny, warm, and dry. The commotion surrounding Dog #63 had thrust Craig unwillingly into the natural world.

As he walked along the edges of Fagin's Resort, he noted the tightly manicured grounds bereft of weeds and most other prairie life. Several stiff topiary trees flanked the entrance to the mansion. Concrete planters held colorful plants that would only last for the summer, being out of their natural range. He noticed that the thick, green, high hedges looked like they were die-cut with nary a leaf out of place. Every evidence of plant debris had been raked off the property and removed. It was like an artificial estate on a film lot. Few bees and birds frequented the property. There were no animals rustling in the brush since there was no brush.

It was a long walk around Fagin's Resort to The Wishing Well, but he and Wags saw no one on their journey. Wags wondered what he was going to do with her. At least he'd taken her away from the Cruikshanks. Still, knowing he was their nephew was not comforting.

Craig had struggled thinking about what he was going to do with her. If he set her free, she could run off and get lost or hit by a car, or worse yet, be found by Uncle Francis. He might have wished these dire outcomes for Dog #63 before, when his laptop fell on the floor and broke. Now, he felt differently. He realized that it wasn't the dog who'd caused all the trouble, it was his uncle in his never-ending quest for more money. Nothing was ever enough for Cranky Franky, who would squish anyone and anything that got in his way of making more of it. He expected others to do the work it took to get more money. He hated it when his workers erred, like Craig did, but he could always fire him, hire someone else, and move on. That's exactly what old Cranky Franky would do.

Craig knew that there would be no back pay and no employment in the future. Although he had hated the job, the money kept him in computer games and upgrades. Having been computer-free for a week, however, he discovered that he actually could live without one. He wasn't sure at first, but when he was looking for Wags, he'd noticed the late-summer monarch butterflies that populated the Wishing Well property. They fluttered around the prairie flowers on Brambles' Sward—purple coneflowers, black-eyed Susans, and zinnias—lighting atop them to draw out their nectar.

He was curious about them, so he looked them up in an old set of encyclopedias his parents had in the basement. Craig liked what he learned: that butterflies were incapable of biting because once they morphed from caterpillars to butterflies, their jaws were gone, leaving long, curled proboscises like drinking straws to take in their liquid diet of nectars. Dogs could and did bite, cats could scratch, and humans could do the unthinkable, so butterflies seemed perfect to him as they were lovely beings that didn't bite or kill anything to survive. They were pretty things that circulated among pretty flowers in a happy circle. Wanting to know more about them, he momentarily rued the loss of his computer, but he had managed to fit in a visit to the library to use their computers while he was hunting Dog #63 in town. His research whet his appetite for more knowledge about butterflies.

All these thoughts flitted in his head as

he, with Wags still struggling in his arms, passed by the lush lilac bushes that signaled the beginning of the Wishing Well property. Maybe there were other species of butterflies he could find there . . .

Meanwhile, the Tiggywiggles and their allies in the search for Wags were becoming worried and discouraged. Nobody gave voice to the possibility that Craig really had "gotten rid" of Wags. With her indominable spirit, it would be hard to believe any harm could come to her, but they knew that even she was no match for large, disreputable human beings like Francis and Cookie Cruikshank.

· · ·

"Where could he have taken her?" Bea asked her uncle Brambles as they stood in a small meadow in the woods dappled with sunlight.

"I wish I knew," said Brambles, "but we haven't covered all the trails yet, so let's keep searching."

"Yeah, let's go," Auggie agreed, running ahead.

. . .

Billy was scouring Endwell and coming up with nothing but dead ends. He stopped the car at an overlook of Sioux Creek and got out for a breath of fresh air. *Oh where, oh where, can my little dog be?* he thought, realizing that he'd come to think of her as *his* dog. She was an entertaining character, Hortense and the kids loved her, and she was the only cure for his bombastic snoring. Yes, they had to find her.

. . .

Hortense nervously busied herself about the kitchen, cleaning every nook and cranny and reorganizing the pantry to keep fear from overtaking her. She was carefully combining two half bottles of vanilla when she heard a soft knock at the door. She felt deflated, knowing that anyone who found Wags would be bursting into the house with lots of barking and exclamations of joy. *Who could this be?* she wondered. *One of those home repair companies soliciting my business? Not now! Of all times!*

She slogged to the door and opened it to Craig Cruikshank with Wags in tow. The nanosecond the door opened, Wags flew like a missile into Hortense's arms. Wags was so wiggly, Hortense couldn't hang on to her. Wags sprung out of her grasp and sprinted to a far corner of the house under a couch, hiding from her captor.

"Craig!" said Hortense, astonished by his arrival and Wags's return. "We thought . . ."

"That I was gonna get rid of her . . ." said Craig.

"Yes," Hortense breathlessly interjected.

"That's just what I'm doing. You can have her! That'll burn Uncle Frank's shorts."

"What? Oh, come in and tell me all about it," said Hortense.

The humans went into the kitchen and

took seats around the kitchen island. Wags remained unreachable, observing the scene from afar under a low sofa where she would be impossible to extract.

"Wags, come here, sweetie pie!" said Hortense, who wanted to hug and kiss her.

Wags didn't move, not trusting her safety with that nasty human Craig in the house.

"OK, you'll come out when you're ready," Hortense said to Wags. Turning toward Craig, she said, "What made you bring her here?"

"It's a long story . . . got any coffee?" said Craig.

"Coming right up. I'm all ears."

Wags was grumpy because now that she'd gotten back where she belonged, Craig, wouldn't leave. She was grunting growls in his direction, sounding like a Geiger counter. With coffee steaming from their cups, Craig told Hortense the saga of Dog #63.

"So, Uncle Cranky won't pay me what he owes me, I can't afford another computer, and he wanted me to get rid of her," he said, finishing his story. "I couldn't hurt her, so I thought of the one thing that my uncle would hate the most: giving her to you, the Tiggy-wiggles. He hates you all."

"I think he hates everyone, and probably down deep even himself," said Hortense. "We can't thank you enough. The gang'll be home soon, and I don't want to spoil the surprise by calling them." Then she called to the dog in the distance under the couch, "Wags, you naughty girl. You were at least partially, although not purposefully, responsible for the demise of Craig's computer." Looking back at Craig, she said, "We'll replace your computer, of course, but if there's anything else we can do ..."

"Well, there is one thing ..." said Craig as the pup formerly known as Dog #63 burst out from under the couch and raced to the door at blinding speed. The door opened. Wags barked and jumped up and down in pure bliss as the search and rescue team returned.

"Wags!" said Auggie.

"You're back!" said Bea.

"A story with a happy ending! My kind of

story!" said Brambles, lightly pushing through the entrance with Wags and the kids jumping as though they were on a trampoline, sharing enthusiastic hugs and kisses. Nomad circled around and around with joy at the sight of his friend home safe and sound.

"Craig thought the meanest thing he could do to his uncle was to give her back to us! Isn't that wonderful? It *is* amazing!" said Hortense.

"Thanks, Craig," said the kids almost in unison. They continued to heap praise on him until embarrassment creeped up his neck in a red flush and he begged them to stop.

"Enough!" Craig had to speak up to be heard over the cacophony of happy voices.

The door opened again, and Billy entered. He was immediately besieged with love from all sides. "Whoa, whoa, whoa! Looks like our dream's come true! Wags is back!" He issued a deep sigh of relief. Turning to the boy, he said, "Is this your doing, Craig?"

Hortense answered for him, "Yes, darling, it is!"

"What can we do to repay you?" Billy asked.

"It seems that Wags played a role, unintentionally of course, in breaking Craig's computer . . ." said Hortense.

"Time for an upgrade, Craig," said Billy. "Whatever you'd like. Anything else we can do?"

"Well, yes, there is," said Craig tentatively. "I've decided to go to school for . . ."

"You'll have a great future in computer science, and we'll make sure your tuition is paid so you won't graduate in debt," said Hortense.

"Actually, I'm thinking of something else," Craig admitted reluctantly. "Since I've been without a computer and searching for that little mutt, I've discovered nature and have decided to become a conservation biologist. I found out that many of the plants and creatures in your prairie are endangered. I want to help keep our ecosystem healthy, so I'd like your permission to study the wildlife at The Wishing Well."

"Of course, of course," said Hortense and Billy on top of one another.

"I can show you all of nature's sacred places here," said Brambles.

"We know lots about nature too," said Bea.

"Wow," said Craig. All sorts of dreams were coming true at once.

There was a relieved moment of silence before Bea piped up again. "But what about all the other dogs at the puppy mill? What'll happen to them?" she demanded to know. Wags, now safe herself, worried about Kind Kirby and the other dogs.

"We have to do something!" Auggie said urgently.

"My uncle always told me that puppy mills were not illegal," said Craig.

"But animal cruelty *is*," said Brambles. "And those poor animals are probably being mistreated."

"Yeah," said Craig. "With all that's been going on, I don't think Uncle Frank and Aunt Cookie will find anyone to give them food or water or wash down the kennels. They wouldn't consider doing any of that themselves."

"Let's go get 'em!" cried Bea. Her brother added an enthusiastic "Yeah!"

"They'll never let us past the gate," said Brambles. "We'll have to call Sheriff Deck.

. . .

Billy placed the call to Sheriff Dimonte Deck.

"You need proof they're running a puppy mill?" Billy said to Sheriff Deck on the other end of the line. "The kids saw it, and Craig confirmed it. Oh, right. What to do with the dogs . . ."

"We'll take 'em!" the kids shouted loudly so Sheriff Deck could hear them.

"Well, I guess they'll need someplace to go . . ."

Billy was drowned out by voices shouting their approval.

"I've got an idea," Craig said several times until the group could settle down enough to hear him.

Chapter 18

Cranky Franky Plays Chicken

At Fagin's Resort, Francis and Cookie were packing for a spontaneous trip to Pulao that Francis had announced out of the blue. He'd gotten a call from his cousin, Craig's mom. Playing both sides of the situation, she said that her son had told her that he was planning to help the Tiggywiggles shut down a puppy mill at Fagin's Resort. She'd over-heard it at The Dandy Diner when she was picking up hamburgers for herself and tuna sandwiches for the cats. She still thought she could garner lucrative favor with her stingy, old relative.

Cookie and her husband could've flown

halfway around the world on the fuel of Franky's anger alone.

"I *am* hurrying, Cranky, er Francis!" said Cookie. "What do you think, the blue or the pink outfits? Pink, yes, we'll be in the tropics."

Francis snorted his frustration.

Cookie fretted. "Are you sure the Cruikshanks will take Ani and Vladi? They have an awful lot of cats, and Ani has allergies ... I don't know ... and what about The Dogg House? I guess Craig'll have to take care of it all until we get back ... but do we even know where Craig is? ... True, he can't be far, but still ..."

Cookie was flustered with her husband's snap decision to go on the vacation she'd longed for. Now she was in full-blown panic mode having to move so quickly under pressure. She hated having to rush anything, especially her wardrobe decisions.

Now Cookie growled and snorted. A fine vacation this would be if she forgot the right shoes or jewelry for each outfit. Francis had insisted that they could buy anything they needed there, but Cookie just wasn't sure that she'd find just the right accessories on an island so far from the nearest Nordstrom. How long would it take to get there if she ordered something on Amazon? Too many questions. Too little time.

Francis had decided on the trip when Mrs. Cruikshank called. She hadn't seen Craig all day, but her friend Drucilla Sorenson, the neighborhood hall monitor, had called to say she'd seen Craig walking up the drive to The Wishing Well with a squirmy, little dog in his arms, confirming what she'd heard at the diner. The Tiggywiggles were nothing but trouble. Francis hated trouble. For Cranky Franky, it was time for a long overdue vacation.

. . .

Sheriff Deck was sitting in his squad car outside The Dandy Diner, savoring a leisurely cup of coffee and a triple berry scone, when he got the call from Billy. Sarge, Deck's drug-sniffing chihuahua, snapped to attention, hearing Sheriff Deck's voice darken with concern, and pounded on his kennel in the passenger seat. Sarge loved his work and was ready for action. Sheriff Deck was alarmed and angry to find out that a puppy mill had been operating under his nose. He would take care of it! He turned on his lights and sirens as he sped through town toward Fagin's Resort.

. . .

Francis paced as Cookie packed. She seemed to be in slow motion, and he was steamed. He wanted out of the whole dog business altogether. Cookie didn't notice him slipping out and heading for The Dogg House.

Standing in the doorway of the barn, Francis considered his investment and his profit margins. The dogs were barking and howling. Would they ever stop? What was their problem? He decided to fix it so they'd never bark again. He flicked his lit cigar toward a soggy, old bale of hay and headed for the garage.

He got in the lowrider that was souped-up for speed and leaned on the horn until a frazzled Cookie waved from a window. Moments later, she appeared, carrying their bags. Out of breath and wheezing, she shoved them into the car. This was not the way she wanted to start a vacation!

. . .

The gang at The Wishing Well had now turned their attention to the dilemma of the remaining dogs at The Dogg House. They decided on a game plan. Brambles would lead a reconnaissance party through the woods to find the gap in the back fence that Craig had discovered when he was looking for Wags. Hortense and Billy would meet Sheriff Deck at the gate to Fagin's Resort to make a reasonable request of the Cruikshanks that the dogs be released to them.

Brambles, the kids, and the dogs dashed off across the prairie now cloaked in twilight, with Craig bringing up the rear.

Hortense and Billy took the Range Rover, rushing west toward their unfriendly neighbors. As they pulled up next to the squad car in front of the mansion, Sheriff Deck was talking into the squawk box.

"Mr. Cruikshank, it's Sheriff Deck. Please open the gate. I need to talk with you. Francis? Cookie? Open up now!"

Sheriff Deck got no response. Although it seemed hopeless, Hortense, once again the diplomat, got out of the car and rushed to the speaker at the gate. "Please, Francis and Cookie! It's Hortense and Billy from next door. Please open the gate!"

Abracadabra, like magic, the gate opened. The lowrider with Francis and Cookie inside whooshed past the sheriff and the Tiggywiggles, burning rubber on the pavement. Hortense and Billy ran on foot into the property through the gate that was closing. Sheriff Deck jumped back into his squad car and spun it around. With lights and sirens blazing, he followed the Cruikshanks, who were speeding toward the highway.

. . .

The rescue team pressed their way into the woods in the waning light of the day. Flying through the brush, Auggie caught his toe on a branch. He went airborne into a thicket of leaves and thistles. "Your hair is so full of brambles, I guess we'll have to call you Brambles Jr. from now on," chuckled Brambles, hoisting his nephew out of the undergrowth.

"Where do we go now?" Bea said urgently.

"There's a path along that stand of pines that'll take us in the right direction," said Craig in hushed tones. Wags and Nomad knew the way, taking the lead. The others hurried close behind. Pine needles scratched their faces but made a cushy trail on the ground. The scent opened up their nostrils and reminded them all to breath. Their anxiety had almost overwhelmed them.

. . .

"Bea and Auggie said that The Dogg House is at the west end of the property beyond the garages," said Billy, who was now all in favor of the quest to save the dogs.

"Let's hurry so we can get the dogs out before Cranky Franky and Cookie come back," Hortense responded, trotting in the direction of the kennels.

"I don't think they'll be coming back anytime soon," said Billy, hustling along with his wife. As they hurried back through the barnyard, the high-pitched howling of dogs filled the air with an odd crackling noise in the background.

. . .

At the far edge of the pine forest, Craig took the lead to find the hole in the fence. It wasn't easy with only the rising moon as their flashlight. The rest of the crew kicked into the brush along the base of the fence to find the opening. Wags and Nomad ran back and forth, anxious to free their friends. Then Wags started digging. Leaves flew back in her wake. Craig came over and found the rusted, bent part of the fence. It was a squeeze, but Craig pulled it up so they could all get through, and they took off running toward the barn. Brambles, now winded from the exercise, brought up the rear.

A crackling sound caught their attention. Then, a flash of flames. A twig of hay had sparked from the smoldering mess Cranky Franky left behind. The barn was on fire!

. . .

When Hortense and Billy got to the barn, they gasped at the smoke building in intensity. The single spark had set dry bales of hay afire. Still, they rushed forward to save the dogs.

Hortense worked to open the cages on the bottom. Billy unlatched and took dogs out of the top row of kennels. Soon, dogs were swarming about, running in all directions. Flames were beginning to run along the floor of the barn toward Hortense and Billy.

"We've got to go," said Hortense.

"I've still got a bunch to go . . . you go . . . now!" said Billy.

. . .

Hortense was guiding dogs out of the barn with the help of a couple of shepherding Shelties when the rest of the team arrived. The flames were now licking the side of the building.

"There's a hose on the other side of the kennels," Craig shouted. Like one of the brave warriors in his Mineshaft game, he ran into the barn past Billy, who was emptying the last of the cages. "Go!" he shouted to Billy.

Billy, his arms full of little dogs, dashed out of the barn.

The kids and Brambles corralled dogs as they fled from the barn in a panic. Wags and Nomad ran nervously in circles, checking to find all their friends.

Craig found the hose, turned it on, and began to douse the fire as best as he could.

In this game, he was shooting for the highest level: saving all the dogs.

. . .

"What'll we do with all these dogs?" Hortense shouted.

"Take them to the garages," Brambles said. "The door's open. Let's go."

Covered in canines, Hortense, Bea, and Auggie ran toward the garages. Auggie turned back.

"What about Craig?" Auggie shouted above the riotous noise.

"I'll get him!" Billy shouted, unloading his cache of dogs on the ground and dashing back to the barn.

. . .

Wags and Nomad had surveyed all the dogs coming out of the barn. No Kirby!

"Where's Kind Kirby?" Wags cried.

"He must still be in there!" Nomad said as

they rushed back into the barn just as Billy was going to get Craig.

"Craig! Get out of here! We got all the dogs," Billy shouted. "Let's go!" Craig couldn't hear him and kept trying to save the barn with a gush of water that was no match for the fire.

. . .

"Kirby!" Wags called out. "Kirby!"

"There he is!" Nomad spotted Kind Kirby cowering in the back of his cage, too afraid to come out since he'd never left it before except for mating.

"C'mon, Kirby! Run!" barked Wags. She and Nomad were circling and barking at the base of the cages.

"C'mon, Wags!" Billy said, trying to get the excited dog to follow him. She continued circling and barking toward Kirby's cage. Nomad was howling, afraid they wouldn't get Kirby out in time.

"Craig! Let's go!" Billy shouted to the back of the barn. "There's no saving the building!" Craig finally dropped the hose and began to run out. Billy noticed Wags and Nomad whining and howling near the kennels. He spotted Kind Kirby crouching back in his kennel, rushed over, and pulled the shivering dog out of the cage. "We'll get you outta here, old boy!"

They all dashed out of the barn through a shower of sparks. Just as they had gotten to safety, the roof crashed down and the walls caved in.

Wags was ecstatic. "Saved!" she roared. Spinning around Billy, who had Kind Kirby in his arms, she barked "Saved!" again and again.

Hortense closed the garage door to keep the dogs in. Then she, Brambles, and the kids sprinted from the garage to the barnyard. Nomad rushed toward Brambles with such vigor that they ran into each other and collapsed together on the ground. "Saved!" Brambles hollered. "Good boy!" he said to Nomad, and then to Billy and Craig he said, "Good boys!"

Everything seemed to stand still for a

moment. The adrenaline rush passed. The humans gathered into a circle with Wags, Nomad, and Kind Kirby in the middle for a group hug. Craig stood uncomfortably off to the side until Brambles grabbed him firmly by the arm and pulled him into the group. Dogs, humans, and friends together. Family.

. . .

While the barn burned to cinders, Sheriff Deck followed Francis and Cookie, who were driving at warp speed toward the airport. He hoped to catch up to them without causing an accident along the way. Francis, the car lover, handled his vehicle like a race car driver pushing the pedal to the floor. His car vanished into foggy dips in the road and then reappeared on the rises. This was the ride of a lifetime for Francis. He couldn't have been happier. Cookie was terrified. She screeched epithets she'd never said aloud before. "Yikes, Franky! We're gonna die!"

The highway was Francis's old stomping

ground. He and his high school friends used to play the game of chicken on this route. Late at night, when there was no one on the road, two cars would face off a quarter of a mile apart and then speed toward each other until one of them, the chicken, swerved out of the way. It was Cranky Franky's favorite game. He won every time. The sheriff hoped it wouldn't come to that tonight.

. . .

Kind Kirby leaned against Billy's legs. He'd always feared humans, but Billy was the one who had saved him. Billy's heart had melted at the sight of poor Kirby shivering in his cage, too afraid of humans to save himself from the flames of an oncoming inferno. He picked up the little fellow, and Kirby clung to him for dear life, with his claws curling like fingers into Billy's shoulder.

"Looks like you've got a new friend," Hortense said mirthfully to her dog-hating husband.

"*Temporary* new friend," Billy responded with a question in his voice.

"We'll see," Hortense said. Turning to the group, she said, "Now what? Uncle Brambles?"

"Ordinarily, I'd have suggested we give them all a bath, but there are too many of them for that. We'll need to get them out of Fagin's Resort before Cranky Franky and Cookie get back."

"With Sheriff Deck on the case, they won't be back soon," said Billy, now hugging Kirby.

"Uncle Brambles is right," said Auggie urgently. "We can't just leave them here."

"We could put them in our garage at The Wishing Well until we can find homes for them all," Bea suggested.

"We'll call Faith to see if she can round up a crew to help," Hortense offered. "In the meantime, we can keep them in the garage at night and let them out onto the luring course during the day. Good thing we didn't take down all the fencing yet."

"Whoa, whoa, whoa!" said Billy loudly to

pierce the chatter of the group avidly planning for the dogs of The Dogg House. "I never said that The Wishing Well could become a dog sanctuary!"

"Indeed you didn't, dear," said Hortense sympathetically. "Let's be democratic and put the matter up for a vote. Who's in favor of creating a *temporary* dog sanctuary at The Wishing Well?"

All except Billy enthusiastically shouted their support with "Ayes" all around.

"Who's against it?"

"Oh, all right, I can see I'm outnumbered," Billy said dejectedly. "But remember, it's *temporary*. Only *temporary*."

"Sure thing, Dadoid," Auggie said cheerily.

"We'll find them homes," said Bea, "eventually . . ."

"We'll need to get a convoy of vehicles together for the transport," said Brambles.

"I'll drive!" Bea enthused.

"Not until you have your driver's license, honey bunch," Billy said firmly.

"Craig, would you please go get the car,

and we can load it up with as many dogs as we can fit in it and take them home . . ."

"Sure thing, Mrs. T.," Craig said, trotting off toward the gate.

"I'll help," said Billy, following Craig with Kind Kirby still nestled in his shoulder.

"Well," Hortense said to Bea and Auggie. "Your dreams have finally come true! You got your own dog and then some!"

. . .

Sheriff Deck lost sight of Francis and Cookie when Francis took an abrupt sharp turn to the right. Cranky Franky thought he'd lose the law by speeding down the familiar back roads, heading east toward the airport. Deck radioed his husband, Norbert Dingle, who'd been chatting with Deck when he was diverted to Fagin's Resort.

"Norb, we've got a problem," Deck exhaled in a rush.

"On it," Norb responded in a flash when Deck spewed out the details.

. . .

Norb was ready for action since Dimonte told him that the Cruikshanks were up to something. He did not like the idea of his husband facing off against his high school rival who was devious and mean. He knew that Cranky Franky would stop at nothing if challenged. Like Francis, Norbert knew all the highways and byways around Endwell. When Dimonte called, Norb jumped into his car before Dimonte could finish his sentence and drove like lightning to help his husband.

. . .

As Francis and Cookie charged on, the lights and sirens of Deck's squad disappeared behind them. Cranky Franky didn't need night vision scopes to find his way. He sped up. The car flew off the hills and then bounced down into the deep depressions in the road, scraping the fenders. Sparks flew. "EEEEEEK!" Cookie shrieked, sure that they were going to flip into a ditch. For Francis, it was better than fireworks. His eyes narrowed and his lips curved upward into a menacing smile.

Norb knew that Cruikshank was a creature of habit without ingenuity or creativity. County Trunk XX was an old, rutted route once used as the road to the airport. Norb sat on Highway C, which intersected with XX about five miles east of Endwell. As Francis appeared, flying down a hill, Norbert pulled out and parked across the road just over the rise and waited, too scared to breathe.

"Nooooo!" Cookie screeched. Francis caught sight of Norb's SUV right in front of him. Seeing the face of his nemesis in his headlights, he sped up, threatening to T-bone him. Valuing his own life more, Cranky Franky jerked the steering wheel sharply to the left just inches away from Norbert's driver-side door. The lowrider fishtailed into Norbert's SUV, sailed over an embankment next to the road, pitched downward into a ditch, and then bounced up and hobbled over a rocky field. It jolted to a stop when the tires blew out with a loud *whoosh*. It was the first time Cranky Franky had ever lost a game of chicken. He was flushed with wrath.

Cookie sobbed with relief that they survived what could've been a fatal crash. Her mascara dripped from her eyelashes. Her nose was bleeding, and she was too overwhelmed to worry about her clothing. She lifted up her designer shirt and used it as a towel to wipe away the blood and tears.

Norb was deeply shaken. His air bag had deployed into his face, knocking him backward in his car that was still parked in the middle of the road. He let his breath out in huffs, realizing how close he'd come to the end.

"Norb? Norb?" Sheriff Deck was shouting to his husband over the radio. "You OK?"

"Yeah, sort of," said Norbert, still breathless. "Franky and Cookie crashed into the Honeyacre's field. I better get loose from this air bag and go check on 'em."

"Oh no you don't," Deck said, seeing Norbert's SUV in the distance. "You hold tight until I get there. Cranky Franky might just have a gun in his belt."

He threw the microphone to the floor, sped toward Norbert, and jumped out of his car as he came to a screeching halt.

"OK," said Norb to no one, sinking back into his seat. His rush of adrenaline dissipated as he slowly began to breathe normally. "All right."

. . .

Francis and Cookie were both in shock. Sitting in their crumpled classic car, staring into the dark field, Cranky Franky was lurid with rage. He should've killed that nuisance Norbert Dingle! *What a loser. He wrecked my car,* Francis thought bitterly. Norb was the same as ever. Dumb. Righteous. Hero. For the first time in his life, Francis was the chicken. He hated Norbert and his obnoxious husband for it. They got into things that weren't their business. He'd get them somehow, but he was just too shaky to think of that something in the moment.

"I think I broke something!" Cookie whined to her husband. Her pink travel outfit was ruined. "Frank? Frank? What'll we do now?" Francis was fuming, groping for a cigar in the glove compartment. He found one, dug a lighter out of his pocket, and lit it. He sucked it in deeply, expelling smoke that filled the interior of the car. Cookie, who was allergic to cigar smoke, threw up in his lap.

...

Sheriff Deck and Norbert carefully approached the Cruikshanks' vehicle. Francis's reckless driving was enough for Deck to take him into custody. Cookie, suspected as Cranky Franky's accomplice in the puppy mill, was charged as well. He handcuffed them both and shoved them into the back of the squad. Deck was securing his prisoners in seatbelts when Sarge, whose kennel had popped open in all the confusion, leapt out, ran around, and sunk his teeth into Francis's ankle. "Arrrrrgh!" Francis exploded with a litany of impolite epithets. He pulled on his restraints so fiercely, he almost broke loose.

"That'll do, Sarge," Deck said with a voice that suggested approval. He picked up Sarge and encircled his arms around his dog and his husband in a grateful group hug.

. . .

Late that night and early the following morning, all the regional news outlets ran stories about the noted local couple arrested for animal cruelty. Cranky Franky looked dark and surly as usual, scowling in his mug shot. Cookie, the media star, was barely recognizable with her blood-streaked face devoid of makeup, one earring missing, and a mat of unruly straw for hair.

Chapter 19

All's Well That Ends Well in Endwell

The next day, the smell of fresh, moist grass and happiness filled the air at The Wishing Well. By midmorning, the sun, dazzling in a China-blue sky accented with cheery nimbus clouds, burned off the dew.

The property seemed to be as crowded as it was during Frenchy's Woofstock. Several dozen former denizens of The Dogg House were playing in the fenced-in luring course. Patience and her colleagues from the Doggo-Rama Sanctuary, Dog On It, and the ASPizzaCA were entertaining them with pizza-shaped rubber toys. Now that they were fed, watered, and washed down with the garden hose, the dogs were happily enjoying their freedom. Other volunteers were working diligently to match dogs with collars and leashes donated by Faith Carmichael. Faith was on her cell, calling all her customers to help find foster homes for the pups until they found their *furever* homes.

Extortionist Love Puppy had set up their band under a drooping oak tree. They were playing an acoustic set of puppy love songs. Big Mama Wysywyg sang "How Much Is That Doggie in the Window?" Toothless Walter smiled broadly, strumming his accompaniment. Felonius Hunk took the day off from playing piano and was sleeping under a willow tree, snoring louder than Big Mama was singing. Hortense, Bea, and Auggie sat on a picnic bench, singing along. Billy, Brambles, and Craig stood chatting with Sheriff Deck and Norbert Dingle.

Wags, Nomad, Kind Kirby, and Sarge relaxed by the pool, gnawing on elk antlers from the Au Naturel Pet Store. Sarge was particularly aggressive with his, popping up now and then to growl it into submission and then plopping back down to chew on it. Kind Kirby, who'd never had toys before, looked to Wags and Nomad for direction. They dutifully showed him the way by chewing their own antlers. Kirby nibbled on the tip of his, then tested it with his teeth, then began to gnaw it like the others.

People hovered around a table laden with Finessa Bopp's phenomenal apple fritters and carafes of coffee and orange juice. The mood was jubilant but relaxed in joyful communion.

"I propose a toast!" Brambles said, summoning everyone's attention.

"What with, Uncle Brambles?" Bea asked, joking impertinently. "We don't have any toast!"

"Hmmn," Brambles murmured, smiling. "Gather ye round, everyone, and get a *cup*."

When the majority had followed his instructions, he continued, "Let's raise our toast in honor of the dogs who brought us all together today."

"And the humans too!" said Auggie, who'd chosen to raise his apple fritter for the toast.

"Everyone deserves a toast!" said Hortense, raising her coffee cup.

"Here! Here!" they shouted together.

"There, there!" Bea cried gleefully.

They sipped their drinks and nibbled their sweet rolls together, laughing and talking about their triumph over evil.

When the chatter simmered down, Billy asked Dimonte the question that was on everyone's mind. "What's the news on Franky, er Francis, and Cookie, Sheriff Deck?"

"Francis is not talking. Not a word. We charged him with animal cruelty, but he won't confirm or deny it. I'm charging Cookie too as co-conspirator. They're in our jail for the time being. They'll be going away for a long while."

Norbert said, "And oh, get this! Cookie, er Empress Cruikshank, ordered an organic green spirulina smoothie with kale, apple, and banana for breakfast this morning!"

"She *got* bologna and cheese on white,"

Dimonte interjected, giggling and snorting orange juice. "Too much! It's too much!" Getting more serious, he added, "She only ate the cheese, of course, and you know what that means!" He and Norb collapsed into one another, laughing. The others joined in the mirth.

Looking at his family and the group as a whole, Billy said, "You've all turned my life around. I always said no dogs, and now we have dozens . . ."

"For the time being," Hortense interjected.

"Nonsense!" he said with mirth.

"Oh, Dadoid, after all we've put you through, do you still love us?" said Bea doubtfully.

"Hold on a minute, honey bunches of groats . . . let me check." Billy consulted his phone, swiping through several screens and pondering a bit. "Wait a second. Oh! Yes, here it is! It seems that I *do* still love you," he said, unreservedly happy.

"And what about Wags?" Auggie wanted to know.

"I'll have to check. Hold on. Checking . . . checking . . . checking . . . Good news! It turns out I love her too!"

"And Kind Kirby?" asked Bea.

"Yes! I love *everybody* on this glorious day!" said Billy.

"And we love you, dear Billy," Hortense cooed with their children jumping in to agree.

"Now I have a toast!" Billy said. "To Wags Tiggywiggle, for freeing herself, all the other dogs, and most of all me from my hatred of dogs!"

With that, Wags barked "I love you too!" and jumped into Billy's arms, where she had started becoming a Tiggywiggle in the first place, and licked his face with joy.

Coda

The Tiggywiggle family adopted Wags and Kind Kirby, both of whom clung to Billy throughout their adoption ceremony for family and friends later that week.

Brambles Wysywyg formally adopted Nomad and several more of the rescued dogs from The Dogg House, having gotten permission from Billy Tiggywiggle to expand his canine family. As the former partner of Francis Cruikshank, he was interviewed by many news outlets. The stories generated commissions for a dozen new statues of dogs by owners across the country, including one from Governor Dorinda Feathercloud, who wanted one of her own faithful dog, Thunder.

Faith Carmichael, Patience, and the volunteers of Doggo-Rama Sanctuary, Dog On It, and the ASPizzaCA found foster and *furever* homes for rest of the dogs freed from The Dogg House.

Mr. Armstrong adopted a roly-poly, fawn-colored pug from the group of rescues. He named her Ella. Louie fell in love with her, and they planned to practice agility and painting together.

Craig Cruikshank signed up for all the science classes he could at Endwell High, having learned that he'd need a background in biology, chemistry, zoology, ecology, and conservation work to achieve his goal of becoming a lepidopterist (a scientist that specializes in the study of moths and butterflies). In his free time, he roamed the woods with Brambles and the kids to observe the fauna and flora of southeastern Wisconsin. He used his top-of-the-line smartphone to capture their images and his new computer to track his findings.

Francis Cruikshank went to prison for animal cruelty, where he studied various new avenues of criminal enterprise.

Cookie Cruikshank was sentenced to three years at a women's prison as her husband's accomplice in the puppy mill business, a charge she vehemently denied. Her loud, constant complaining about the lackluster diet and lack of cosmetics in prison earned her a single-occupancy cell reserved for inmates who lacked the social skills to room with another inmate.

Ani and Vladi Cruikshank spent little time in the animal control facility where they were taken after their owners went to prison. They were snapped right up by Lydia Déjeuner, who saw dollar signs in breeding them. Putting the two elegant dogs in her car, Vladi bit her on the nose when she said to him, "You're my new baby boy, ooga booga."

Ani peed on Déjeuner's white carpeting immediately upon arrival at her new home.

When he turned up his nose to further breeding, Lydia Déjeuner put Champion Sir Lancelot Lickalot of Lake Lucy up for adoption on Greg's List. Guinevere Rodriguez, a drag queen whose act lacked that certain something, swooped in and took Licky for a handsome fee. It was love at first sight. Queen Guinevere took Licky to Tricks class at the Endwell Kennel Club, where they earned their Advanced Trick Dog title. Guinevere and Lancelot Lickalot went on to headline the drag show at Pride Fest and place third on the America's Winners talent show.

The Tiggywiggles and concerned community members formed a coalition to protest puppy mills. When they testified at the state capitol, Lydia Déjeuner was there arguing that laws against them would unfairly penalize legitimate breeders. The issue continues to be argued.

Sheriff Deck agreed with the Tiggywiggles about puppy mills, but as an officer of the court, he could only enforce the laws, not make or change them. He decided to run for state assembly to have his say as a legislator. He and Norbert adopted their two foster children, LaTasha and Nash, who ran the campaign and generated enthusiastic community support.

The End
(For Now)

Wags's Mental Agility Activities

GLOSSARY

Ameliorate — Make something bad or unsatisfactory better.

Bodacious — Excellent, admirable, or attractive.

Cacophony — A harsh mixture of sounds.

Crampons — A metal plate with spikes fixed to a boot for walking on ice or rock climbing.

Debacle — A sudden failure; a fiasco.

Denizens — Residents, tenants, dwellers.

Detritus — Litter, waste, garbage.

Emanated	Issued or spread out from a source.
Errant	Erring or straying from the proper course or standards.
Esker	A long ridge of gravel and other sediment, deposited by meltwater from a retreating glacier.
Faux	Artificial, fake.
Klieg light	A bright carbon arc lamp especially used in filmmaking.
Lackadaisically	Unenthusiastically.
Levitate	Rise up, float, soar.
Lucrative	Producing a great deal of profit.
Menagerie	A collection of animals kept in captivity for exhibition.
Miser	Penny-pincher, cheapskate.
Mustachio	Mustache, whiskers.
Myriad	Many, numerous.
Nirvana	A state of spiritual enlightenment or bliss.
Noxious	Poisonous or very unpleasant.
Oracle	Prophet, psychic, visionary.

Petulance	Grumpiness, crabbiness.
Reverence	Worship, admiration, devotion.
Savannah	A grassy plain with few trees.
Savvy	Know-how, confidence.
Sloughed	To get rid of something undesirable or no longer required.
Solicitude	Attentiveness.
Soporific	Sleep-inducing, calming.
Sward	Grassy meadow, prairie, or pasture.
Undulated	Rippled.

BOOK DISCUSSION POINTS

1. Describe a character from the book and why you would or wouldn't want to know them.
2. What challenges did characters face in the book, and how did they handle them?
3. Describe a real-life challenge and how it was handled by you or another person.
4. Wags had a dream. What is your dream, and how do you hope to achieve it?
5. What episode in the book stands out to you, and why?
6. Write two sentences using a glossary word.

WRITING, DRAWING, AND SPOKEN WORD ACTIVITIES

1. Create a text to your best friend about your reaction to the book.
2. Create a training manual for dogs and/or humans.
3. Pretend you are a podcast host and interview one of the characters from the book.
4. Pretend you are a travel agent and create a promotional brochure or speech for Endwell.
5. Draw a picture of, or describe, a character or setting that intrigues you.
6. Pretend you are one of the characters and write a diary entry from a key moment.
7. Write a review of the book and send it to Amazon or Share What You're Reading.
8. Write a letter to Wags Tiggywiggle at www. TrickDogBooks.com/connect.